Out

Out

Sandra Diersch

James Lorimer & Company Ltd., Publishers
Toronto

James Lorimer & Company Ltd. acknowledges the support of the Canada Council for the Arts and the Ontario Arts Council for our publishing program. We acknowledge the financial support of the Government of Canada through the Book Publishing Industry Development Program (BPIDP) for our publishing activities.We acknowledge the Government of Ontario through the Ontario Media Development Corporation's Ontario Book Initiative.

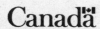 

Library and Archives Canada Cataloguing in Publication

Diersch, Sandra
    Out / Sandra Diersch.

(SideStreets)
ISBN 978-1-55277-421-X (bound).—ISBN 978-1-55277-422-9 (pbk.)

    I. Title. II. Series: SideStreets
PS8557.I385E34 2009   jC813'.54   C2009-901669-9

James Lorimer & Company Ltd.,
Publishers
317 Adelaide Street West
Suite 1002
Toronto, Ontario
M5V 1P9
www.lorimer.ca

Distributed in the
U.S. by:
Orca Book Publishers
P.O. Box 468
Custer, WA USA
98240-0468

Printed and bound in Canada

For Tammy

With special thanks to Ellen, Shelley, and Joan for their suggestions and criticisms. Thanks also to Andree at Maple Ridge Secondary for answering my questions.

Chapter 1

That night, Alex almost didn't notice the couple as they slipped from the building and dashed across the gas station parking lot. They reached a car and the man leaned against it, pulling the woman to him. In the moment before she reached her arms up and draped them around his neck, headlights from a passing car spotlighted them and Alex caught a glimpse of the man's face.

He blinked and shook his head. *No way*. Alex looked again. The car was gone; the couple in shadow again. *That can't be him*, he told himself as he finished filling his tank. He forced himself to concentrate on replacing the gas cap, closing the little door, grabbing his receipt, climbing behind the wheel. He tossed his wallet on the passenger seat and slid the keys in the ignition.

Then curiosity got the better of him and he looked across the street again. The couple had stepped away from each other and the man was holding the car door open. The woman climbed behind the wheel and started the engine. Her headlights came on, bouncing off the building in front of her and reflecting back on the car. The light was so bright it was as though the sun had reappeared.

Alex's hands froze on the steering wheel. He hadn't been wrong. The man leaning in the car window kissing the woman who was *not* his wife was Paul Carruthers, father of his good friend Emma, head of the parish council, practically nominated for sainthood in the Maple Ridge parish of St. Michael's Catholic Church.

With shaking hands Alex started the car, stalling it twice before the engine turned over. His tires squealing on the hot pavement, he sped out of the parking lot. How many Sundays had Paul Carruthers sat in church looking so pious beside his wife, beside Emma and her four brothers and sisters (the youngest of whom hadn't even been baptized yet) while he thought about the next time he'd be able to bang his girlfriend?

A car horn sounded angrily and Alex swerved back into his own lane. Forcing himself to concentrate on driving and *not* what he'd just witnessed, he made his way up the curving stretch of highway. There were fewer houses the farther he got from town, the trees got denser, the night darker. Living in the middle of nowhere — or Whonnock, as Alex's neighbourhood was more commonly known — meant large properties, farms, few neighbours, and dark streets.

Finally he turned onto his own gravel driveway and parked his car beside his mother's van. He climbed out and stared at the low, rambling house. The porch light had been left on for him but Alex was too restless to go inside. Instead he went around the side of the house. The smell of freshly cut cedar hung in the air; his dad must have been working on the deck.

He stared out across the wide expanse of yard, not sure what to do, where to go. And then he noticed the ladder nailed to the thick, gnarled trunk of an old maple, leading up to the tree house. He hadn't been inside for years; they'd even talked about tearing it down, but suddenly that's exactly where he needed to go.

He crossed the grass quickly, climbed the ladder and ducked through the hole in the floor. Once inside he paused to look around. He was tall enough now that he had to bend to avoid whacking his head on the low ceiling. Had it always been so small in here? He glanced out the small window, just a square hole cut in the plywood wall, and he saw the lights from the house, the neatly trimmed lawn, his father's shed.

Alex sat down on the dirty, fir needle strewn floor and stuck his long legs over the open edge of the rear wall. He rested his arms on the two-by-four that his father had nailed across the opening and sighed, trying to make sense of the mess in his head, trying to rid himself of the image of Paul

Carruthers feeling up a woman who was not his wife.

What was the guy doing with a *girlfriend*? What about his wife? What about Emma? An image popped into his head: Emma sticking her tongue out at him as he stood, so serious, helping the priest at the altar. Alex groaned. The two families had been friends for years. What was he supposed to *do* with this information? How was he supposed to face Emma or her parents the next morning at church? Alex clasped his hands together, leaning his forehead against them. He felt the bite of his knuckles.

He didn't need this complication in his life. He was already riddled with doubt and confusion about what he believed. All his life, Alex's faith had come so automatically. He had been told it was so, and he believed completely that God loved him and wanted him to be a good person. He remembered that calming sense he'd always had of being washed clean, of having the chance to start fresh after Mass every week. Now his skin chafed under the Sunday clothes. And each week it got a little bit harder to put on the Sunday façade, to go through the motions like he still cared, to smile and shake hands.

Did Mr. Carruthers' conscience bother him at all when he was handed Holy Communion on Sunday morning? Did he confess, ask forgiveness, promise not to do it again?

Alex stretched his head back, rubbing the back

of his neck with one hand as he stared at the uneven wood panels of the roof. He and his brother Mark had helped design and construct the tree house, and it had always been a safe retreat. How many times as a child had he run to the shelter of its plywood walls? He could see his smaller self climbing the ladder frantically, collapsing to his knees, hands folded: "Please God, you know I'm sorry about cheating on my math test. I promise not to do it again."

He gazed out at the dark, starlit sky. Once he'd felt a sense of release when he'd said the familiar prayers. But in the past few months it had become more and more difficult to just shut down his brain and give his thoughts and needs up to that higher power. He'd lost his certainty that anyone at all was out there. And now, with the image of Paul Carruthers with that woman burned into his memory, how could he go to church and pray and sing when Mr. Carruthers was sitting just across the aisle? How could he ignore what he knew? Say nothing, do nothing? Alex pressed his temples harder against his clasped hands, leaning into the pain, longing for an answer.

Finally he lowered his hands and pulled his feet up. He stood awkwardly, his legs numb from hanging in space for so long. He climbed down the ladder, jumping the last couple of feet to the grass below as he had always done as a boy. Suddenly, Alex felt a longing to be a child again. *When did things stop being so simple?* he wondered as he headed back to the house and crawled into bed.

***

Alex woke Sunday morning to the sound of his father's insistent tapping on the door. For a minute he lay still, one hand on his belly, hoping to soothe the frantic flapping inside him. But finally he forced himself to get up, pull on some clothes, and head to the kitchen. His family was seated around the kitchen table. Mr. Straker looked up when Alex entered the room and frowned.

"We have to get going — I'm reading today," he said.

Alex swallowed hard but forced himself to speak calmly. "I'm not going to Mass this morning."

The skin around his father's eyes tightened. He set his coffee cup down. "I thought you were going to speak to your manager about not being scheduled to work on Sunday morning," he said. "This is the second time in the last few weeks, Alex."

"I don't have a shift, Dad. I've decided ..." He cleared his throat and straightened his shoulders, wishing his father would look away, even for a second. But Mr. Straker held Alex's gaze hard with his own. "Mass isn't doing anything for me. I've decided not to go anymore." The words came out in a flurry of sound and then there was silence.

Mark coughed and Alex's gaze slid to his brother. *You're insane, man,* Mark's eyes said.

12

Alex looked away. Of course Mark would think so. Mark was still an altar server, he still prayed. As far as Alex could see, his brother believed in his heart that his prayers were heard, that *someone* was listening.

"Is this something to do with that girlfriend of yours?" his father asked at last.

"No!" Alex snapped. "This has nothing to do with Laura. She doesn't even know I've been thinking about it."

"Well who then?" Mr. Straker asked, evenly. Anyone overhearing this conversation would have no idea how angry his father was. "Who has convinced you that it's okay to abandon your faith like this? Some of those ball players you hang out with, like Riley?"

Alex let out a slow breath. "There's no one to blame. It's just me." He wished he'd sat down before starting all this. He eyed a chair longingly, but stayed where he was.

"Why didn't you speak to us about your doubts, Alex?" his mother asked, her eyes wide. "We didn't even know you had any."

Alex felt a twinge. He could have talked things over with his mom. She likely would have understood, helped even. But it was too late now. Now everything was tied up with what he'd seen last night and there was no way he could tell either of his parents about *that*.

His father stood and took his cup to the sink. "Yes. Exactly as your mother says, you suddenly

13

announce that 'Mass isn't doing anything for you' the moment we're about to go out the door. What exactly does that mean?" He had turned to face Alex again, the familiar vein on the left side of his neck throbbing. The flapping creature in Alex's gut returned and brought friends.

He scrambled for the words to explain how he felt but they danced away from him, like a prize being held out of reach. "I don't *feel* anything anymore," Alex began. "I sit there every week, and there's nothing. It's all just talk."

"Have you prayed?" Mr. Straker asked. "Have you spoken to Father Birch? What have you done to help yourself?"

"I've tried to pray and I *can't*!" Alex cried, his self-control slipping dangerously away the more his father questioned him. "I don't know how to explain it to you!"

His father opened his mouth but Mrs. Straker put a hand on his arm, stopping him. "We need to go, Tate," she said gently.

"This conversation is *not* finished, Alexander," Mr. Straker said as he left the room behind his wife. With a quick backwards glance at Alex, Mark followed.

Alone in the kitchen, Alex sank into a chair, dropping his head back to stare at the ceiling. Things were getting worse every day. What was happening to his life?

Chapter 2

Alex stretched out alone on the beach towel and closed his eyes, letting the hot July sun beat down on him, calming him. It had been very chilly in the Straker household the last couple of days. Ever since he'd made his announcement on Sunday morning his father had barely spoken two words to him. How long was that going to go on? Alex had a whole year left at high school and he could easily imagine his dad staying cold and aloof the entire time.

He pushed the thoughts of his dad firmly from his head. When Laura arrived, he would have almost the whole afternoon to spend with her, and he was going to enjoy it. Whonnock Lake spread out before him, sparkling in the July sun. The long stretch of beach was dotted with a few families and old couples settled into their lawn chairs, but

Alex had found a fairly secluded little spot to spread their towels.

Laura appeared on the path leading from the parking lot. Alex sat up and leaned back on his hands, watching her approach. He never got tired of looking at her, of hearing her voice. He'd fallen for her, hard, the first time he'd seen her at church almost two months ago.

She'd just moved to Maple Ridge from Coquitlam. That Sunday, Emma Carruthers had brought her friend Laura to the Sunday service — that's where he'd first seen her. "I'm not actually Catholic," Laura had said to him. I'm just … searching." Around them the post-church crowds of people had milled about in the warm May morning but Alex had barely noticed them. He saw nothing but her and the little splash of freckles that floated across her nose.

Watching her now, he couldn't believe she actually liked him. At least one thing in his life was going right. He closed his eyes and grinned into the sun. He could hear her feet on the sand.

"Al-ex," Laura said, tickling his face with her long blonde hair.

Alex opened his eyes, grabbed her, and pulled her down onto the towel beside him. She lay in his arms laughing, her blue eyes hidden behind her sunglasses. Gently, he took them off.

"What were you thinking about?" she asked.

"Not much."

"Really? You sure you weren't thinking of

me?" she asked, running a finger down his arm.

"Well, maybe a little," he whispered, his mouth close to her ear.

"I thought so ..."

He smiled as he felt Laura's skin prickle. They both had goosebumps. He closed his mouth over hers and she responded by wrapping her arms around his neck. He could feel her breast, thinly covered by her bikini top, against his bicep. Alex gazed down at her, lying beneath him on the towel, her skin tanned by the sun, little beads of sweat lining her forehead. Her lips were red and a bit swollen from their kissing.

Alex reached out and, amazed at his own bravery, ran his fingertips slowly down the side of one breast and back up the other side. Laura didn't try to stop him. Instead she slid ever so slightly closer to him. She liked it. Feeling bold, Alex put his hand right on her breast, kneading it gently with his palm. Her nipple hardened and she sighed. Alex rolled on top of her and began kissing her hungrily. He'd never felt like this before, almost sick with desire. It was amazing and terrifying. And Laura was kissing him right back. But he knew he couldn't go much farther ... he'd better slow down. Pulling away, at last, he rested his head on her chest and closed his eyes, breathing heavily.

Laura cleared her throat and Alex pulled away as a family appeared through the trees carrying towels, buckets, and shovels. Laura sat up and wrapped her arms around her knees, grinning sheepishly at Alex.

"When's your next shift at the grocery store?" he asked.

"Tomorrow, eleven to seven."

"Want me to pick you up when you're done?" Alex asked. "We could catch a movie, get something to eat."

"Sorry, can't," Laura told him. "Sam and I are having dinner with my dad."

"Really?" Alex said, unable to keep the surprise from his voice.

In the two months he and Laura had been going together she'd mentioned her father only once to tell him that "the bastard ran off with some woman he met on a business trip." Alex hadn't dared bring the subject up since.

"Yup. He called and asked. Said he wanted a chance to apologize, try to make up for 'lost time'." The words were simple enough but Alex caught the angry undercurrent in her voice.

"That's great that you're giving him a chance," he said hesitantly.

Laura snorted. "I would have told him to go screw himself, but Sammy's really been missing the jerk. I didn't want to disappoint my brother."

"What did your mom say?" Alex had met Mrs. Killeny twice and he liked her. She and Laura were a lot alike.

"Mom said we should go," she said with a smile. "She's been seeing someone she met online, if you can believe it, and now she's all about forgiveness and getting on with life."

"But it's not that easy for you," Alex said.

"We had to move out of our house, Alex," Laura said softly. "Because *he* was having some kind of crisis *we* have to live in a bloody basement suite." She laughed bitterly.

Leaning across the towel, Alex kissed her forehead. "Can't you think of *anything* good that came from you moving to Maple Ridge?" he whispered.

"One or two things, I guess," she whispered back. "We're being watched."

"Then let's give them something to see," Alex teased. "Come on, let's cool off in the lake, and then I have to get to work," he said, grabbing her hand.

Twenty minutes later, they climbed out of the water and grabbed their towels. Alex gazed at the water streaming over Laura's shoulders, down her chest, and cursed the six hours of serving coffee that awaited him, keeping him from her. How had the day gone by so quickly?

"We have to get a move on now," he said, pulling a T-shirt over his head.

"Uh-huh," Laura replied rubbing herself vigorously with a towel. She disappeared under the blue cotton, re-emerging with tousled hair.

"No, I'm serious Laura," Alex said. "I was late twice last week because of you."

Laura lowered the towel. "Because of me? It wasn't me who insisted there was plenty of time for one more round of tennis on the Wii, which, as I recall, I *won*. Isn't there some kind of church penalty for lying, Alexander?" she demanded.

"Penance, actually," he corrected her with a smile.

"Okay, penance. Your penance for lying is to kiss me."

"I've never had this kind of penance before," Alex said and kissed her.

Laura giggled as they began clearing their things. "I guess not, with a priest giving it out."

They threw their things in the back of the car and Laura pulled out of the parking lot. Five minutes later she pulled up the Straker's long driveway and parked in front of the sprawling rancher.

"I like your house," she said. "It looks comfortable. 'Spacious.' Isn't that the real estate word? More spacious than our basement suite, that's for sure."

Alex stared at the home he'd lived in his entire life, trying to see it from Laura's perspective. His mother's flowerbeds bordered the front walk. Planters, crazy with summer colour, dotted the porch, and hanging baskets hung from the eaves. The driveway was packed gravel, which made it easier to drive on when it snowed, but it was a headache to rake when the birch and maple leaves fell in the fall.

"I guess it's okay," he said, reaching behind him for his stuff.

Laura laughed. "You are such a guy, Alex," she said. "I had fun today. Maybe we can do it again sometime?"

In answer Alex leaned over and kissed her. Adjusting themselves around the gearshift, they clung to each other. Alex ran his hands through Laura's silky hair, kissed her lips, her chin, and nibbled her ears.

"Is that your dad?" Laura whispered, pulling away from him suddenly.

Startled, Alex shot a glance toward the house. Sure enough, there was his father standing on the porch watching them.

"I'll talk to you later," he muttered and bolted from the car.

The gravel crunched beneath the tires as Laura backed down the driveway but Alex didn't watch her go. He kept his eyes on the ground in front of him, mounted the two steps to the porch, and headed around to the side door.

"That was quite the performance you and your girlfriend put on," his father said, stopping him. Heat flooded Alex.

"Sorry," Alex muttered.

"I'm a little concerned, to be honest," his dad went on. "You seem pretty serious about this girl, but she's not Catholic."

"No, she's not Catholic, Dad," he said, through a tight jaw, "but she's a nice person anyway."

"I have no doubt she's a nice person. That's not my point."

"What is the point then, Dad?" Alex asked, his voice rising. "I don't want to *marry* her. We're just having some fun, enjoying each other's company!"

"There's no need to yell, Alexander," his dad said calmly. "It's the 'just having fun' I'm concerned about. It's easy to get swept away by lust."

"Yeah, I'm sure. You know what, though, Dad?" he said, hiking his sports bag onto his shoulder, the handle tight in his grip, "I'm a big boy now. And I can make my own decisions about what kind of 'fun' I have. And who I have it with. And I think I can control my *lust*."

His father gazed at him impassively. He let his eyes slide slowly to the handle in Alex's clenched fist and back to his face again. "Can you?" was all he said before he walked down the porch steps and disappeared around the side of the house.

Chapter 3

When Alex left the bathroom fifteen minutes later, he nearly collided with Mark. He hadn't seen much of his younger brother lately, which was as much Alex's fault as it was Mark's. They were always going in different directions. Alex looked his brother up and down. Had the kid gotten even skinnier? And what was with the pale skin? Did he ever see sunlight?

"What are you staring at?" Mark demanded.

"Do you ever eat?" Alex asked. "Or go outside? You look sick."

"I guess I should look like you? Mr. Buff? Head as thick as my legs?" Mark narrowed his eyes, daring his brother to reply. Instead, Alex continued down the hall to his room.

"You going to work?" Mark asked abruptly, stopping Alex before he shut the door.

"Yeah, why?"

"Could you give me a lift into town?" Mark was blushing.

Alex roared with laughter. "You've got a lot of nerve asking for a ride after insulting me," he told him.

"Yeah, well, you insulted me first."

"Be in the car in ten minutes," Alex said and shut his door.

Mark was already in the Corolla when Alex made it outside. Alex glanced at him as he slid behind the wheel and started the engine. Did the kid ever wear anything but black? And what was with the *jeans* on one of the hottest days of the summer? He rolled his eyes as he backed down the driveway.

"Radio working?" Mark reached for the dial. He turned the knob but eventually gave up as nothing but static came through the speakers. "When are you going to get yourself a decent sound system?" he muttered. He turned his head to look out the window.

Alex didn't bother to answer. He wasn't really interested in starting anything with his brother. Not that Mark was much of an opponent. He was a lot like their dad that way, keeping his anger tightly controlled. He had slouched down in his seat with his feet up on the dashboard.

"Where am I taking you?" Alex said.

"You can drop me outside Cooper's Drugs."

"Going to get yourself a job?"

"Don't start with me, Alex," Mark snapped.

"What am I starting? I just asked a question."

"Well stop asking questions, okay?" Mark told him. "Just mind your own business."

Irritation flared in Alex. "You might want to be a bit more polite to the guy you're always begging for a ride, Markie," he said, using the childish nickname.

"Sorry," Mark muttered, sitting up. He couldn't seem to stay in one position for more than a couple of seconds. Alex glanced over at the clenched fists tucked between his brother's knees.

"What's up with you these days, anyway?" he said.

Mark searched Alex's eyes, and it was really clear — he wanted to say something. Instead he looked away again. "You wouldn't be interested in my problems, Alex," he said at last.

"You never worried about whether I was interested or not before," Alex teased him. "Remember all the times you dragged me out to the tree house so you could tell me something super-important?"

The little brother he remembered was always yakking someone's head off about something or other. Nowadays Mark didn't share much of anything. Most of the time, if he was home at all, he was locked in his room. He scowled all the time and he barely spoke.

"We're not little kids anymore," Mark said. "And it's not like you share with me, either." He was talking about Alex's refusal to go to church.

"I guess some things are just too difficult to

explain," Alex said, pulling the car to a stop outside the drug store.

Mark grabbed his backpack and climbed out. He leaned back in the car window.

"Would you be able to pick me up later?" he asked.

Alex rolled his eyes but nodded. "I'm off at eleven."

"Yeah, that's fine. Here's the address," Mark said, tossing a folded bit of paper on the passenger seat. "Thanks, for the ride. And thanks for ... asking ..." he trailed off awkwardly.

Alex watched his brother walk away, his backpack slung over one shoulder, his hands stuffed deeply in the pockets of his jeans. It wasn't until Mark finally turned a corner and disappeared that Alex pulled away from the curb and continued on his way to work.

He pulled up outside the coffee shop a few minutes later. It wouldn't have been his first choice of employment but he'd needed a job, and his boss, a friend of his dad's, had needed help. Alex usually smelled of coffee when he was done but at least he didn't have to wear a stupid paper hat and a hairnet. And the clientele tended to be a bit older and more mature than the fast-food crowd, another bonus.

Around ten that night, he heard a girl's voice.

"Hi, Alex."

He looked up from the steamer to see Emma Carruthers standing in line with her boyfriend,

Riley. At the sight of her, Alex's heart beat a little quicker.

"Emma, hey," he said with a nod and a quick smile. "Hey, Riley."

As his friends placed their order at the till Alex took several deep breaths and focused on the job in front of him. He hadn't seen Emma since seeing her dad with another woman. Alex tried to look calm, but he wasn't.

"Feel free to make mine extra good, Alex," Emma teased a few moments later.

"Right," he replied, glancing up quickly. He caught Emma's quick wink and then she whispered something in Riley's ear and disappeared to the restrooms. Riley leaned against the wall as he waited for Alex to prepare their order. Alex and Riley had known each other since elementary school. They'd been altar servers together, had played on the same ball team, had camped out in the tree house. Alex had introduced Riley to Emma. They were his *friends*. Alex didn't know what to do about what he knew.

"Haven't seen you lately," Alex said. "Having a good summer?"

"Can't complain," Riley said with a grin. He grabbed a couple of straws and beat out a rhythm on the counter.

"How're things in the *real* world?" Alex asked slyly. When Riley had graduated from high school in June he'd gone to work for his father.

"Let me tell you, Alex my man, full-time

sucks," Riley said with a violent shake of his head. "You don't know how lucky you are still getting by on part-time. My dad is even making me pay *rent*. Can you believe that?"

"Giving you a real taste, eh?" Alex said with another chuckle. There were some pluses to being stuck in high school for one more year.

"Well, it'll be worth it when I buy my car this fall," Riley told him with his usual take-it-as-it-comes attitude. "So, how are things going with Laura?"

"Good. She's great."

Riley chuckled. "Never thought you'd finally get up the nerve, Straker."

Alex placed their order on the counter. "Two tall skinny vanilla lattes, extra whip," he said. "Never thought I'd see Riley Jacobs in a shirt and tie every day, either."

"Well, you haven't yet, and if I have anything to do with it, you never will."

"Riley, did you ask him yet?" Emma asked, joining him at the counter. She turned to Alex. "Has Laura talked to you about the four of us getting together?"

"Not sure," he hedged. He kept his eyes focused on the steamer.

"I'll email you, we can set something up," Riley said. "Speaking of emails — did you get that email about the pickup game Saturday?"

"Yeah," Alex said, glancing at the order for the next customer. "You going?"

"Thought I might show up, yeah," Riley said. "Be good to throw the ball for a while."

Alex nodded. "See you Saturday then."

Emma threw him a smile and a little wave as the two of them moved away from the counter. She seemed so carefree. Alex went sadly back to foaming milk for the next order.

At ten-thirty his supervisor told him to pack it in early. "I'll close up tonight," she said. "Go home."

Alex didn't need to be told twice. He tossed his apron in his locker and headed out to his car. It wasn't until he was pulling on his seat belt that he remembered Mark. He flipped open his cellphone and punched in his brother's number.

"You've reached Mark's voice mail. Leave a message."

"Mark, it's Alex. I got off early and I'm on my way." He snapped his phone shut and started the car.

Alex parked in front of the apartment building and shut off the engine. It was only ten-forty. Alex sighed. Knowing Mark he'd show up at ten past eleven and not a minute sooner. Alex leaned the driver's seat back, crossed his arms, and relaxed, letting his eyes close.

Low voices and a sudden quick laugh jolted Alex and he opened his eyes. Two guys were walking in from the road. Alex sat up, recognizing Mark. He didn't know the other kid. He glanced at the dashboard clock and saw that it was eleven fifteen. *Jerk*, Alex thought, reaching for the keys as the boys reached the front steps of the apartment building. He was about to honk the horn when the stranger suddenly hugged Mark. Currents of unease darted through Alex as he watched his brother accept the embrace.

Alex leaned hard on the horn. Both boys jumped and Mark's buddy disappeared up the steps and into the building. Mark trotted over and climbed silently into the car.

"You don't have to be so polite, Markie," Alex said as he pulled out of the parking lot.

"What's that?" Mark stammered.

"Next time he tries that crap on you," Alex said, "just shove him away."

"Me shove Scott? He's as big as you," Mark said with an uneasy laugh. "Don't worry about it, it's nothing."

"I'm just saying," Alex replied.

Chapter 4

The ball sailed through the cobalt sky and landed with a satisfying *thwack* in Alex's glove. The runner slowed, turned, and headed back. Alex fished out the ball and shot it to Kyle Jeffries at second base who sent it back to the mound. It was hotter than hell in the ballpark but Alex didn't care. He adjusted his cap, wiped the sweat from his forehead, and smiled. It felt amazing to be out on the field, the warm leather of his glove like a second skin on his hand, the sun beating down on his head. Next summer he'd definitely sign up for summer league, he told himself as the pitcher sent the third out back to the dugout. He hustled in with the rest of his team, tossed his glove on the bench, and grabbed a bat from the stack.

The next batter was up. Matt Dawes.

"Come on Dawes, Take your time, buddy," Alex called. He tapped his bat against his cleats, moving from one foot to the other. The pitch came; Matt Dawes leaned in, connected, and sent the ball soaring into the outfield. Alex watched, knowing it was out even before the centre fielder caught it.

Alex got into position at the plate. He swung the bat a couple of times, getting the feel of it, eying the pitcher warily. The first pitch was a foul, the next two were balls. Alex held his ground, waiting for the right moment. He'd know it when it came.

"Strike two!" the umpire called, snapping his gum. "Shoulda swung at that one, Straker," he said.

Alex stepped out of position, loosened his shoulders and stretched his neck. He took a quick look around, clearing his mind. He was just about to step back to the plate when he saw her, Laura, sitting on the grass behind third base. She caught his eye and smiled, gave him a tiny wave. Alex grinned back as the blood pounded in his ears. He stepped to the plate and got into position, struggling to keep his thoughts on the pitcher in front of him and not on the gorgeous blonde watching him.

He struck out spectacularly, swinging so hard he fell to the ground in a cloud of dust. Jeers filled the air as he headed back to the dugout.

The game ended twenty minutes later with Alex's team losing by one run.

"You going to get something to eat?" Riley asked.

"Guess so," Alex said, throwing gear in his bag.

"Can I catch a ride?"

"Sure. Just gotta check in with Laura. Give me a second."

Laura was standing by the bleachers waiting for him. Alex's heart leaped. She wasn't waiting for Kyle or Matt or any of the others, but for *him*. He grinned at her.

"The guys are going for something to eat," he said, "but I could blow them off and we could go do something together."

Laura shook her head and gave him a rueful smile. "I've got to work at five. But we're going hiking tomorrow, right?"

Alex nodded. He held her eyes, unable to look away.

"And can we set something up with Emma and Riley?" she said. "Emma keeps asking but …"

"Hey, Straker, you comin' or what?" Riley called, drowning out the rest of her sentence.

"I've got to go."

"Aren't you going to say goodbye?" Laura whispered, catching his arm.

He kissed her and pulled away, then kissed her again, harder, before he sprinted off. He and Riley tossed their gear in the trunk of the Corolla and climbed in.

"I'm definitely springing for an air conditioner when I get my car," Riley muttered, cranking open the window.

Alex backed out of the parking lot and headed down the highway. "Just one more thing to get fixed when it breaks," he said.

"You know what, Alex?"

"Yeah, I know, you don't care."

Riley reached into his bag and pulled out a bottle of water. "So how're things going?" he asked between long sips. "Emma tells me she hasn't seen you at Mass for a few weeks."

"No." Alex knew his absence would not go unnoticed.

"Bet your dad is thrilled," Riley said with a chuckle, finishing the last of his water. "Is he talking to you yet?"

"Not if he can help it," Alex admitted, pulling to a stop at a red light. He watched a father lead his small son across the street, his hand tight around the little boy's. A small sigh escaped him.

"Has he blamed your 'defection' on me?" Riley asked. "We lapsed Catholics are a real bad influence."

Alex pressed the gas and moved through the intersection. "Yeah. Laura, you, and the guys on the team, you're all responsible," he told him. He glanced over at Riley and smiled.

"It must be great to go through life never having a doubt, or a question about God or faith, eh?" Riley said, drumming his fingers on the door. "Is he pulling the guilt thing on you?"

Alex pulled into a parking spot outside the burger joint and turned off the car. He turned to face Riley. "He's trying," he said. "I wish he'd stop with his questions. The more questions he asks the harder it is to answer them, know what I mean?"

"Yeah, I do," Riley said. "My mom was the same when I stopped going."

"Any advice?"

"Sorry man, wish I had answers for you," Riley said with a shrug.

"Thanks for nothing, Ri," Alex said as they climbed out of the car and headed into the noisy restaurant.

Riley laughed, slugging him in the arm. "Anytime, Alex. Anytime."

They got their burgers and went out to the patio where the rest of the team was gathered around a picnic table. Alex slid onto the bench and set his tray on the scratched wooden surface.

Kyle Jeffries came outside a second later and grabbed at Matt Dawes's fries.

"Get your filthy claws outta my food, Jeffries," Matt said, snatching his tray out of reach.

"Aw, come on Dawes," Kyle whined. "Didn't your mother ever teach you to share?"

"There's room at that table," Matt said, indicating a table occupied by an elderly couple. "Why don't you go sit with them?"

"Naw, I'm going to sit right here beside Alex. Maybe he'll share his fries with a buddy."

Alex shifted over on the bench as Kyle dropped down beside him. He caught Matt's sympathetic look across the table and shrugged, resigned. He could put up with Kyle Jeffries and his big mouth and loud opinions for a while. Thankfully, base-ball practice and games were the only contact Alex had with the guy.

"How's it going, Straker?" Kyle asked around a mouthful of burger. Alex's burger. "That was some strikeout. You been practicing?"

"Naw, just lucky I guess."

Kyle grinned at him. "Watch this," he whispered under his breath. "Hey, Dawes," Kyle shouted. "Isn't that your sister?" As Matt swung around to look, Kyle grabbed his container of fries and sat down again.

"That wasn't my ..." Matt began and then stopped when he saw what Kyle had done. "Jeffries, you fag, stay out of my food!"

"Who you calling a fag?"

"Why else would you keep stealing my food?" Matt asked. "You must have some serious feelings for me."

The guys around the table erupted in laughter. But Kyle glared. Matt stood up and came around to their side of the picnic table.

"I feel the same way," Matt said, putting his arms around Kyle. Kyle threw him off, sending Matt stumbling backwards.

"Get the hell off of me!" he cried, jumping from the table. He spun around, fists up, his face purple with rage. Everyone knew that look well enough. Jeffries could never control his temper. Instantly two guys leaped from their seats and grabbed Kyle's arms.

"Aw come on, Kyle," Riley said easily, "Relax, would ya? Matt didn't mean anything — he was just having a laugh."

Kyle shook off the guys holding him back. He grabbed his ball cap from the cement and brushed it off. "I always knew you were a pervert, Dawes," he said. Shooting one last hostile glance at Matt, Kyle headed for the exit.

"That's okay, sweetheart," Matt jeered as the door swung shut behind him. "We can talk later."

More laughter. Alex laughed along with the others. But the image of his brother *not* shoving Scott away popped into his head.

Chapter 5

Alex woke up to the sounds of the regular Sunday morning activities of his parents and brother as they prepared to go to Mass. The urge to stay in his room until they were gone was strong, but Alex forced himself out of bed. Far better to show his face, show he was doing nothing wrong by not going to Mass, whatever his father thought.

"Morning, Mom," Alex said as he came into the kitchen. "Hey," he added with a nod at his brother. Mark looked up from the newspaper and grunted a response.

"Good morning, love." His mother smiled at him. She finished the last of her coffee and put the mug in the dishwasher. "Sleep well?"

"Yeah. Is there any of that grapefruit juice left or did Mark drink it all?" he asked, grabbing a glass from the cupboard.

"A bit," Mrs. Straker told him. "Are you hungry?

Do you want me to fix you something before we leave?"

"No, I'm —" Alex began.

"Alex can get his own breakfast, Joanna," Mr. Straker interrupted from the doorway. "We need to go. You ready, Mark?"

"Yeah," Mark said, but he didn't get up.

"Good morning, Dad," Alex said, sliding onto a chair at the table.

"Morning," his father replied coolly. "Obviously you haven't changed your mind."

"No, Dad," Alex said.

"You're making a mistake," his father told him.

"Maybe," Alex replied evenly. "But it's my mistake."

"I thought your mother and I had done a better job than this," Mr. Straker went on. "I thought we'd raised you right."

"That's perfect, Dad, pull out the guilty parent card," Alex snapped. He glared at his father. "Maybe this has nothing to do with you or Mom. Maybe this is my struggle, my problem."

Mr. Straker opened his mouth and Alex braced himself for what would come next, but in the next instant his dad closed his mouth again, drawing his lips into a thin line. Without another word he turned and left the room.

Alex stared at the glass on the table until the glass and the table blurred and his eyes watered. Mrs. Straker finished loading the dishwasher then crossed the room to the door. She paused for a second, then turned and came back to where Alex was sitting.

"It'll get easier," she whispered, laying a hand on his shoulder. She leaned over and kissed the top of his head.

"Let's go, Joanna," his father called from the front room.

Kissing him one last time, Mrs. Straker hurried out of the room. The front door opened and closed. The lock clicked. The van's engine roared to life and wheels crunched gravel as they backed down the driveway. Alex breathed deeply then drank the entire glass of juice in one long swallow. When did it get easier? It had been three weeks since he'd made his decision, and his father was still pissed off.

Alex wished he could fast-forward through time to the point where his father had forgiven him. To a place where the temperature didn't drop several degrees anytime they were in the same room. Why did the guy have to take it so *personally*? Why couldn't he just let Alex make his own decisions? He slammed around his room, yanking open drawers, banging closet doors.

By the time Laura pulled up the driveway, Alex was sitting on the front steps, still fuming. Tossing his pack on the back seat he climbed silently in beside her, barely acknowledging her greeting.

"You okay?" she asked, glancing at him as she turned out onto the main road.

"Yeah, I'm fine."

There was a pause. "You don't seem fine," she pressed.

Alex didn't answer her. He jabbed at the controls, trying to get the air conditioner blowing.

Laura pulled over to the side of the road and stopped the car. "Maybe this isn't a good idea," she said, staring out the front window.

Alex closed his eyes, let out a long breath, then opened his eyes again and put a hand gently on Laura's arm. She turned, to look at him.

"Why don't you tell me what happened," she suggested. "Maybe you'll feel better."

"I'm fine. Sorry I was being a jerk," he muttered, finally finding the right button. Cool air blasted into the car, taking the edge off his anger. Laura was still watching him and he forced himself to smile at her. "Honest, I'm fine now."

With a small shrug, Laura started the car and pulled carefully onto the road again. Twenty minutes later Alex directed Laura to the parking lot at the base of his favourite trail in Golden Ears Park. They climbed out of the car and stood for a minute, breathing in the fresh air of the forest.

"You ready for this?" Alex asked at last, sliding his hiking pack onto his back.

"Yup," she said.

He slid his cap on his head, then made sure his note that explained where they'd gone, when they'd left, and who exactly was hiking, was visible through the windshield. Laura locked the doors.

"All these precautions?" Laura asked, slipping

her hand into his. "Where exactly are you taking me?"

"A lot of hikers don't think about it," Alex explained. "But what if one of us falls? Or we get lost?" He stopped when he caught sight of her amused face. "Sorry," he muttered sheepishly.

"No! Don't be sorry, Alex," Laura said, squeezing his fingers. "It's good that you're cautious. Besides," she went on, "you're kind of sexy when you're serious."

His whole life people had been trying to get Alex to lighten up, to stop taking things so seriously. "Gotta learn to laugh at yourself, Alex," his grandfather had always told him. But Alex had never been able to do that, until he'd met Laura. Somehow when she teased him it didn't feel like an attack. He leaned over and kissed her smiling lips.

He led the way into the trees. At first the trail was too narrow for walking side by side, and steep enough to make it difficult to carry on a conversation, but eventually it branched out slightly at the top of a little rise and Alex moved instantly to walk beside Laura.

They wove their way through the towering firs and cedars, following the trail as it wound its way up the side of the mountain. Once or twice they passed other hikers but mostly they had the trail to themselves. They hiked for over an hour, saying little. Alex was not sorry for the quiet. He relished the physical activity, the hard burn of his leg muscles.

The more he worked his body, the less his mind had to do. It was a welcome relief.

Eventually they heard the sound of rushing water and came upon a large creek running down-hill. The trail continued over the creek and disappeared into the trees on the other side but, with quick, silent agreement, they found a moss-covered log and sat down.

Alex pulled out his canteen and took a long, deep swallow, closing his eyes as the cool liquid slipped down his throat. Beside him Laura did the same. He set the canteen down and began pulling food from his knapsack, bags of trail mix, sand-wiches, two apples, a couple of granola bars and some cookies.

"That's a lot of food," Laura observed with a giggle.

"It pays to be prepared," he told her, offering her a sandwich.

They finished eating, slid off the log to rest against it, and sat watching the dance of the water. Laura bent her knees to her chest and wrapped her arms around them. She rested her head on the tops of her knees and looked at him sideways. The tilt of her head made her blonde hair fall partly across her face, hiding her from him. Alex reached out and tucked the hair behind her ear.

"That's better," he said.

He slipped his arm around her shoulders and she nestled in closer to him, resting her head on his shoulder. "How did dinner with your dad go?"

he asked.

"It was okay, actually. Well, a little awkward, especially at the start," Laura told him. "But he seemed sorry."

"And?" Alex said. "You going to see him again?"

"Yeah, I guess." She looked up at him and smiled.

He held her close, wondering when things would improve between him and his own father. They sat like that for a long time in silence.

"Alex?"

"Uh-huh?" he said, rousing himself from the half sleep he'd fallen into.

"I have something to ask you."

Alex sat up straighter, alarmed by Laura's serious tone. "Ask."

"Would it bother you if I went to Mass sometime?" she blurted, her tanned skin turning pink.

Caught off guard by the question, Alex didn't answer immediately. Did he mind? He thought for a second and was reassured by the answer.

"No," he said, then repeated, "no, it wouldn't bother me at all."

She was studying him, looking for signs that he was lying. Alex smiled at her. "Honest. If you want to go, you should go," he said, reaching for her hand. "It's okay."

"I just feel like there has to be something *more* to life. I mean, doesn't it make sense that there's a larger plan? That someone is looking out for us?"

She stopped speaking and looked at him. "Is that what you're struggling with?"

"I don't know if I've stopped believing completely in God," Alex said slowly. "I don't want to *not* believe. I ... I used to sense that *someone* was listening when I prayed, but I don't get that anymore and I don't know why."

"That must feel very lonely," Laura said, wrapping her arms around him.

"You want to walk any further?" Alex asked at last, pulling away from Laura to stand up. He adjusted his cap, cleared his throat.

Laura stood up beside him, brushing the bits of leaf and dirt off her shorts. She glanced at her watch. "Naw, I think I'm good for today. And besides, I'd like to go home and shower before I meet your parents tonight."

Alex rolled his eyes. He would have put off having Laura meet his parents forever if it had been up to him.

"I'd like to meet them, Alex," she said. "Let them get to know me."

"We've only been seeing each other for a few months," Alex reminded her. He was hesitant to expose her to his father right now.

She laughed at the stricken look on his face. "I'm not afraid of them, Alex," she reassured him. "They're not going to scare me away. And I promise to use my fork and not wipe my mouth on my sleeve."

But Alex couldn't laugh at her teasing. "It's not

you I'm freaked about, Laura. My dad hasn't been exactly warm and cuddly lately. Not that he ever was, really, but he's even more prickly now."

She stopped refilling the pack and came over to him, slipping her arms around his waist. "It's going to be *fine*, Alex. Relax, would you?" She gave him a little shake. "You've really got to try not to be so uptight."

He raised his eyebrows at her. "They're not *your* family," he reminded her.

"No, but I do have one of my own, and trust me, my grandmother can give anyone a run for their money."

They gathered up what was left of their lunch, slipped their packs on, and headed back down the mountain.

Chapter 6

Alex couldn't remember ever being as nervous as he was waiting for Laura to arrive at the house later that afternoon. Who knew what kind of dumb-ass thing his father might come out with, what embarrassing questions he might ask. And Mark. Alex shook his head. *If* his brother could pull his act together long enough to be civil it would be a bloody miracle. The kid had been begging for a fight for days, blowing up at the slightest provocation, storming around the house.

Alex looked in the bathroom mirror, scowling at his reflection: Short blonde hair, square jaw, smallish ears, thick neck. Nothing special. He smoothed the front of his cotton shirt down then ran a hand over his smooth chin, trying to decide if he should shave again.

"You gonna be in there all freakin' afternoon?" Mark asked, banging on the door. After taking several deep breaths Alex opened the door and stepped out. As he stepped past his brother Mark gave him the once-over.

"You were in there all that time," he said scornfully, "and this is the best you can do?"

Mark slammed the bathroom door shut and Alex was left alone in the hall. He shot the closed door a one-finger salute just as his mother came out of her room. She gave him one of her "must you?" looks and continued down the hall to the kitchen. Alex followed her.

She began pulling plastic tumblers from a cupboard and setting them on a tray. Alex slid onto a stool at the island and watched her. He would stomp Mark if he was even a little rude to Laura. Alex wondered if he'd been that horrible when he was sixteen.

"You could help," his mom suggested, raising her eyebrows at him. He looked blankly at her. "Cutlery, plates ..." she prompted.

Grudgingly he got up again and started gathering knives and forks.

His mom had just taken the tray outside to the deck when the doorbell rang. Alex sprinted for it, not wanting Laura to be met by anyone but him.

She looked up at him with that smile, her blonde hair held back with a narrow band, falling loosely over her shoulders. She was dressed in a crisp, sleeveless white blouse over striped capris.

"Man, you're gorgeous," he whispered, grabbing her hand to pull her inside. She blushed then looked down at herself.

"This outfit is okay, then?" she asked. He nodded and she breathed out. "Good. I wasn't sure."

"You weren't sure?" Alex parroted. "I thought you were always sure."

Laura laughed. "Well, I try to make people *think* that. So, where are the dragons?" she asked.

Holding tight to her hand, Alex led Laura through the house and onto the deck. His dad had only finished building it that week and the scent of cedar was strong in the air. His mother's flower baskets and planters were arranged around the perimeter and in the middle stood a large table surrounded by cushioned chairs. His parents stood as he and Laura came out the door.

Alex made the introductions and Laura took it from there. She was so easy, so natural and calm. She laughed easily and often, and Alex could see his father responding to her, see his normally stern attitude softening.

"Alex tells me you only just finished building the deck, Mr. Straker," Laura was saying, walking around eagerly. "It's gorgeous."

"Thank you, Laura," he said almost bashfully.

Was his father actually *blushing*? Alex stifled a chuckle as he exchanged looks with his mother. She had noticed too, judging by the small smile on her lips.

"And the flowers are amazing!" Laura was saying, accepting the chair Mr. Straker held out for her. "Did you plant all these yourself?" she asked, turning to Alex's mom.

"I did. I love gardening," she answered, now refusing to meet Alex's eyes. "Do you garden, Laura?"

Alex poured iced tea into two tumblers and handed one to Laura, then sat beside her, close but not touching.

"I love to when I have a chance. But we don't have a garden now. Are those peonies growing by the hedge?" she asked.

In no time at all Laura and his mother were chatting like they'd known each other forever. Alex sat quietly, listening. It was a gift, really, the ability to make small talk. He didn't have it. His dad didn't have it either, he realized, glancing at his silent father. Did his dad struggle for the right words the way Alex did? He'd never given it any thought before, the idea that they might be alike in some ways. He shifted uncomfortably in his chair and took a large swallow of his iced tea.

The kitchen door slid open and Mark appeared dressed in a dark purple T-shirt – *Purple, there's a change for you,* Alex thought wryly — and black jeans, damp hair hanging in his eyes, shoulders slumped.

"There you are!" Mrs. Straker cried, too cheerily. Mark ignored her and headed straight for the basket of crackers on the table. He grabbed a handful before he turned and nodded at Laura.

"How's it going?" he muttered.

"Good," she said with a smile. "It's nice to see

you again."

Mark dropped into a chair, moving it slightly away from the others. He stretched his legs out in front of him and stared at the cedar planks, his dark hair falling over his face. And just like that, the easy, happy mood of the afternoon had darkened. Alex glared at his brother, seething.

Laura casually rested her hand on his arm and rubbed her fingers gently back and forth, setting the small hairs on end, calming him with her touch.

"Did you find the CD you were looking for the other day, Mark?" she asked.

Mark's head snapped up and he stared at her, frowning. Laura laughed. "I was in the mall with my friend Emma. I saw you in the music store. You and your friend were listening to something."

A small smile played at Mark's lips. "Yeah, we found what we were looking for," he admitted. "Took Scott forever to make up his mind, though."

"I can never decide either," Laura said. "I usually just listen to the radio. My brother, Sam, on the other hand, has this huge collection. Took four boxes to pack it all when we moved. I keep telling him to just download music, but he refuses."

Mark sat up and leaned forward. "Oh yeah? What kind of music is he into?"

It didn't take long before she and Mark were yakking away like old friends. Alex grabbed a handful of crackers and leaned back in his chair,

51

his eyes on Laura. She was amazing. No one had managed to drag his sullen, angry brother out of himself for weeks, but here, after barely ten minutes, Laura had him *laughing*.

Laura leaned forward in her chair. "What a beautiful cross, Mark," she said, pointing to the silver crucifix hanging from Mark's neck. He took it off and handed it to her, laying it in her palm. "Oh, it's heavy!" she cried. "Isn't it uncomfortable around your neck?" She handed it back to him, then slid back in her chair and reached for her tumbler.

"No. It's reassuring," Mark told her, staring at the cross for a second before slipping it back over his head.

Mr. Straker got up and started the barbecue. Then he and Mrs. Straker disappeared into the house. Through the kitchen window Alex caught them standing, heads close together, observing Mark with Laura.

"So, have you been back to church since we saw you that time?" Mark asked.

"Mark ..." Alex warned.

"No, it's fine, Alex. I don't mind," Laura said, then turned her attention back to Mark. "I haven't, actually. But I'd like to go. Alex and I were talking about it this afternoon. I really liked Father Birch's sermon the time I went with Emma. He's a good speaker."

"Yeah, he's pretty cool," Mark agreed. "Makes God seem more like He's someone you can talk to who really listens, you know?"

Mr. Straker came to the sliding door holding a plate of seasoned steaks. "Can you put these on the grill, Alex?" he called.

Alex got up and took the plate from his dad, one ear still on the conversation taking place at the table. He opened the lid of the barbecue and dropped the steaks onto the grill. They sizzled and spat as they hit the heat. He closed the lid and sat down again, reaching for Laura's hand.

"There's a great youth group at St. Mike's," Mark said, leaning forward in his lawn chair.

"Emma's mentioned it." Laura sipped at her iced tea, shooting Alex a quick smile. "Maybe I'll check it out some time."

"Did you know that Mark wanted to be a priest when he was ... what, about twelve?" Alex asked, looking at his brother. Mark's face clouded over.

"Don't remember," he said.

"It's true. He looked into seminaries and everything. Do you still want to be a priest, Markie?" Alex teased.

"Sure, maybe," he muttered, standing. "Better than doing nothing, like some people," Alex heard him say as he went back into the house.

Chapter 7

Monday morning Alex woke late. He sat up, put his pillow behind his back, and leaned against the headboard. On the opposite wall was the floor-to-ceiling bookcase his father had built him, filled to overflowing with his trophies and awards. For as long as he could remember he'd felt most happy when he could run, throw, or catch a ball, skate until his heart threatened to burst out of his chest.

Mark liked to tease him, call him a dumb jock, all muscle no brain. But Alex didn't think he was a dumb jock. He didn't do that badly at school, as long as no one asked him to speak in public or describe what he felt. He wasn't a straight-A student like Mark, but how many of those did the world need anyway?

Between two of the trophies lay the crucifix he'd received at confirmation, and beside it leaned the white, leather-covered Bible from his first Holy

Communion. Alex stared at the two objects, realizing, with a jolt, that that's all they were to him, objects. Would it come back? That sense of peace, of *completion* he'd felt at Mass, knowing that God was out there, somewhere, hearing his prayers, guiding him, helping him. Or was it gone for good?

He ground the heels of his hands into his eyes, shook his head. His brother hadn't lost his faith, Alex knew. Sometimes as he passed his brother's bedroom door he could hear Mark praying. Mark had always been a far better Catholic than Alex. Serving at the altar, praying, never missing a Mass. Even when Alex's faith had been intact, there had been Sundays when the call of the ice rink or the ball field had been stronger than the call of God.

Tired of his thoughts, Alex swung his long legs out of bed. He slid into some shorts, pulled a T-shirt over his head and went out to the kitchen. His mother was sitting at the table, cookbooks spread out before her. She looked up from her reading as he came in.

"Good morning, Alex," she said with a smile.

"Hey, Mom." He grabbed himself a bowl, a spoon, milk, and cereal and sat down at the table.

"What are you up to today?" Mrs. Straker asked.

"Not much. Laura and I are going to Whonnock Lake for a while," he told her. "And I have a shift later."

"Good. You can serve Tammy and me your best

chai lattes." Mrs. Straker grinned at him, her blue eyes flashing behind her glasses.

Alex rolled his eyes. "You couldn't go to one of the other two hundred coffee places in town?"

His mother got up from the table and tucked her cookbooks back on the shelf. "Now why would we want to do that?" she asked. "I always try to support my sons."

Alex snorted. "Actually, you're just supporting my boss," he told her.

"True," his mom said with a laugh. "But we're coming anyway."

Alex lifted the bowl to his lips and downed the last of the milk. Wiping his mouth with the back of his hand, he got up and took his dishes to the counter.

"In the dishwasher, Alexander," his mother reminded him.

"Yeah, yeah."

"Alex?" she said. The playfulness was gone from her voice, replaced by a serious tone. Alex stopped and turned to face her.

"What's up?" he asked.

His mother ran her fingers over and over her shopping list, her face creased in a frown. "Have you noticed anything unusual about your brother's behaviour lately?" she asked, her voice low.

"You mean aside from the fact that the kid never gets off the computer?" he said. "He's the only guy I know who's paler now than he was in February."

"That's not exactly what I meant, Alex," she

said. "He was so distant and, and *angry* at dinner the other night."

Alex knew exactly what she meant. "He's a miserable SOB these days," he said. "I've noticed *that*."

"He seems to be really struggling with something," his mom said. She paused. "I've had ..." she began, then paused again. "I overheard him on the phone with one of his friends, and I'm wondering —"

"Well, that's a good sign, isn't it?" Alex said, stopping her flow of words. "If he's talking to someone?" He kept his own face open, hopeful. Finally Mrs. Straker sighed and nodded. "Yes, as long as he's talking to someone."

"I'm sure it's nothing serious, Mom," Alex tried to reassure her. He patted her shoulder awkwardly, but in the next second she had pulled him into a tight hug. Alex stiffened, but then he relaxed into the warmth of the embrace. When was the last time he'd hugged his mother? He was so much taller than her, he could rest his chin on her head. He did, and she laughed softly. She squeezed him one last time then pulled away, wiping quickly at her eyes.

"He really seemed to respond to Laura," she said eventually. "Well, we all did. She's a lovely girl, Alex. Your dad and I liked her very much."

Alex flushed with pleasure, as though he was responsible for how wonderful his girlfriend was. "Dad too? He didn't say anything."

His mom laughed. "When does your dad say anything? No, he liked her. He didn't even seem to mind that she isn't Catholic," she teased.

"Give it time," he teased back, "Dad converted you …"

Laughing, his mother reached up, holding his face with both hands. "Thanks, love," she said and left the room.

Five minutes later, Alex left the house and headed for his car. Cool, damp air met his skin. Frowning, he looked up. The early promise of a sunny day had been broken, thick grey clouds now filled the sky. They'd been lucky to have two weeks of hot, sunny weather, he thought, climbing behind the wheel. Bad weather wasn't a surprise. But it still messed with their plans.

"Guess the lake is out," Laura said, meeting him at the door ten minutes later. "What do you want to do instead?"

In answer, Alex stepped inside and, closing the door with his foot, reached for her, pulling her into a tight, urgent embrace. He crushed his mouth against hers, fitting her neatly against him. Her arms went up around his neck as she kissed him back.

Finally, too soon, Laura pressed him gently away then moved to the kitchen table. Reluctantly Alex let her go. "I got these printed," she told him, picking up a stack of photographs. "They're from our picnic at the lake." She held them out to him.

Alex flipped through them quickly, more eager

to look at the flesh-and-blood Laura standing right in front of him, dressed in a little pink dress, the straps of her bikini tied around her neck.

Tossing the photos back on the table he reached for her again, drawing her to the sofa, pulling her down beside him. "Alex," she said, pushing against him half-heartedly.

He kissed her neck, starting at the spot just below her right ear and continuing down, past her collarbone, to the top of her dress. She relaxed into him; the warm air of her breath on the back of his neck. Running a finger along the flesh just under the fabric of her bikini top, he felt her shudder. He raised his head, grinning.

"Like that?" he asked.

In answer she kissed him hard, then pushed him away. "No more until you answer a question," she said firmly.

Leaning back against the cushions, Alex sighed, resigned. "Okay, what?"

"When can we get together with Riley and Emma?" she demanded.

Alex cleared his throat and studied his hands. "Can't you and me just hang out together?" he asked.

Laura let out an exasperated breath. "What is with you? Why don't you want to do something with our friends? What are you afraid of?"

"I'm not afraid of anything," Alex said, realizing suddenly that he was afraid. "I just don't want to share you."

But instead of lightening her mood, his remark seemed to make Laura angrier. "That's crap!" she snapped. "For God's sake, Alex, I don't get what the big deal is!"

"Sorry," he said, giving in, completely done in by her anger. "Go ahead and make plans with them."

With his words the fire left Laura's eyes and her features smoothed out. Relief flooded him. "We'll have a good time, Alex," she reassured him. "It'll be fine."

"Yeah, sure," he said. But he didn't believe it.

Chapter 8

"Can I get that muffin?" the customer asked.

"Right, sorry," Alex muttered, sliding a pumpkin spice muffin into a small bag.

"I asked for an apple bran, not pumpkin," she said, her voice growing more impatient.

"Sorry." Alex grabbed the apple bran and handed it to the woman, who snatched the bag from his hand and walked quickly away.

It had not been his best day. Alex glanced at the clock on the wall and groaned. As much as he wanted to be done with his shift, he was not looking forward to spending the evening making polite conversation with Emma, trying to pretend he never saw her father cheating.

"What can I get for you?" he asked, looking up at the customer who had just come in.

Laura was standing there smiling at him. His knees went weak at the sight of her and suddenly things were so much better. He smiled back.

"Just this juice," she said, dropping the money into his hand.

"I'll be done soon," he told her, letting his fingers graze hers as he handed her the change.

"I brought my book," she said with another smile as she took her juice and went to sit at a table.

Alex managed to get through the last thirty minutes of his shift without screwing up any more orders and at last he hung up his apron, grabbed his things, and joined her.

"Perfect timing," Laura said, slipping a photograph of the two of them between the pages of her book. "I just finished the chapter. I got a text from Emma," Laura continued. "They'll meet us at that new Japanese place, Tako Tsubo, at six-thirty, is that okay?"

Alex fidgeted with his car keys. He felt Laura's green eyes on him and looked up, forced himself to smile.

"Is that okay?" she repeated. "You did agree to go …"

"Yeah, that sounds fine. Ready?"

He held Laura's hand tightly as they left the coffee shop and headed for his car. They were almost at the restaurant when Laura broke into Alex's thoughts, her hand on his arm.

"You okay?" she asked. "You seem upset about something, uptight."

"You mean more uptight than usual?" Alex

joked, smiling at her. But the effort fell flat.

"Yes," she said, not returning his smile. "Why don't you tell me what's wrong?"

"Nothing's wrong." He smiled hoping to reassure her, but her green eyes pinned him down, like a moth pinned to a kid's science project.

"Don't you trust me?" she asked at last.

"Of course I trust you!" he said, startled by the question. "Where'd you get that idea?"

She was still frowning as she sat back in her seat and looked out the window. "I don't know. Maybe because you never talk to me, never tell me what's going on."

"But there's nothing to tell you," Alex said, scrambling to make things right. He couldn't bear to have her upset with him but there was no way he could tell her why he did not want to spend an evening with Emma Carruthers. "I already told you I'm fine."

Alex could feel the heat of her gaze on him again but he kept his eyes on the road.

"Fine," she said eventually and let the matter drop.

Riley and Emma were already seated in a paper-wall-enclosed "booth" when Alex and Laura arrived. Laura took off her sandals and crawled along the bench opposite Emma. She giggled as Alex squeezed his large frame into the narrow space and sat beside her.

"I'm so glad we finally managed to do this!" Emma exclaimed, grinning at the two of them.

Alex quickly picked up a menu.

"Have you heard much about this place?" Laura asked.

"Emma's parents were here last weekend," Riley told them. "Her dad really liked the octopus."

"Oh, sorry!" Emma cried, then covered her mouth with her hand, her cheeks blazing. "I just remembered. Mom and Dad have finally set Adrian's baptism. It's a week Sunday. I hope you both can come. We're having a lunch at the house afterwards."

"Of course we'll be there!" Laura said, clapping her hands together like a small child while beside her Alex hung his head.

"Yes, Alex, my man," Riley said, misunderstanding Alex's action. "You're gonna have to go to church."

Alex raised his head and tried to laugh with the others. "I'll survive," he said. "So, other than octopus, what's good to eat?"

They ordered, and the conversation flowed, but Alex said very little. He picked at the pieces of California roll and dynamite roll on his small black plate and sipped at the green tea in the little china cup with no handles but he had almost no appetite. Whenever he thought no one was watching he snuck a glance at his watch. Time was standing still.

What would happen to Emma's family when her father's dirty little secret came out? Emma laughed at something Laura said, tossing her head back. She'd be crushed, Alex realized, and the thought made his stomach turn. He and Emma had always gotten along well, had played together as kids, run half-naked through the sprinkler in her backyard. What about her brothers and sisters? And Mrs. Carruthers, what would she do when the truth came out?

Eventually, when they'd eaten what they could, Emma and Laura excused themselves. Alex's muscles relaxed as Emma disappeared through the door of their booth. He took a long drink of water then looked up to see Riley watching him.

"What?" Alex demanded. "Have I got rice on my chin or something?"

"No. Just a bad attitude," Riley told him. "What the hell is with you tonight, Alex? You're dragging everybody down."

Alex opened his mouth then paused as their server knelt beside him and began clearing the dishes. She bowed at both boys silently before backing out of the booth. When he was sure she was gone Alex leaned toward Riley.

"Can I ask you something?" he asked.

"Yeah, what's up?"

"If you knew something about someone —" Alex stopped talking as Riley snorted.

"Sorry, sorry, man," his friend said, covering his mouth. "Just sounded like a bad movie script."

"It is a bad movie script, Ri," Alex told him, and Riley stopped laughing. "I saw something, *someone*, doing something," Alex stopped. He clenched his jaw, fists balled in his lap. "*Cheating.* I saw someone cheating. And I don't know what to do." He looked up, found Riley's eyes on him, his forehead creased.

"It's someone we know?"

"Maybe, yeah. Do I say something?"

"To the person you saw?"

"Yeah. Do I tell him I know? What would you do?" Alex picked up a paper napkin and began ripping it, rolling the pieces into tiny balls as he waited for Riley's answer.

"Geez, Alex," his friend said finally, leaning back against the wall. "I don't know. Maybe it's better to just keep your mouth shut."

"Would you want to know?" Alex asked.

"You mean, would I want to know that I'd been seen cheating? Or that I was being cheated on?" Riley asked.

Before Alex had a chance to answer there were voices beyond the paper walls and then Laura laughed. Alex shot one last look at Riley and then slid down the bench as the girls climbed back in and sat down.

Chapter 9

"We should see about getting you in for your learner's permit," Mr. Straker said, looking pointedly across the patio table at Mark.

"Uh-huh."

Alex reached for the mustard and squirted some on his bun. Slapping the two sides of his burger together, Alex took a large bite and chewed. He and Laura had played lots of Wii Tennis that afternoon, when they hadn't been making out, that is, and all that activity had left him famished.

"Don't want to leave it too long, son," his father went on, "the quicker we get you practicing, the quicker you can get yourself a car, have a bit more freedom."

Mark picked at his hamburger bun and didn't answer. Beside him, Alex caught their mother's anxious frown.

"I could take you in tomorrow morning," she offered.

"Can't," Mark said, glancing up at his father. "Got something to do." He picked up his burger, and then stared at it like he had forgotten what to do with it.

"What do you have to do?" Mr. Straker asked.

"What is this, the inquisition?" Mark snapped, dropping the food on his plate.

"Watch your tone," his father told him calmly. "What have you got to do?" he asked again.

"Just *stuff*."

Alex kept his eyes on his dinner, wishing he were anywhere else. He had to admit that part of him was relieved it was Mark's turn to get the brunt of their father's displeasure.

"We're concerned about you, Mark, sweetie," Mrs. Straker began.

"You go off for hours," Mr. Straker interrupted. "When you're home you're either holed up in your room or abusing the rest of us with your foul moods. I'm getting tired of it. Either tell us what is going on or ..."

"Or what?" Mark asked. Metal scraped against wood as he jumped to his feet, sending his chair crashing to the deck. Alex looked up. "You gonna kick me out? Ground me? What?"

"Mark!" Mrs. Straker cried, reaching a hand out to him. Mark jerked away from her. His dark eyes were wild, his usually pale face even paler as he glared at them all.

"Why don't you all just leave me the hell alone?" he cried, and then he was gone.

Yup, Alex thought, *nothing like eating together as a family. We should really do this more often.* He looked from one parent to the other.

"Tate," Mrs. Straker said gently. "Getting angry isn't going to help."

"I won't stand for this melodrama, Joanna," Mr. Straker told her.

"He's hurting," his wife said, placing a hand on his arm. His father visibly relaxed at her touch, and Alex smiled, glad he wasn't the only one who fell to pieces when a girl touched him.

Alex and his parents finished their meal in silence. At last his mom stood up and began loading dishes onto a tray. His father finished the last of his beer and set the glass down. He stretched out his legs and folded his arms across his chest.

"What are you and Laura up to tonight, Alex?" he asked, all traces of his earlier displeasure gone.

Surprised at being spoken to pleasantly by his dad, Alex stammered out, "Nothing, Laura's out with her mom and brother."

"Your mother and I enjoyed meeting her the other night. She's a lovely girl." Mr. Straker stood up and stretched. "We're going out for a while," he said. "We won't be late."

"Have fun," Alex said, and was still staring long after his dad had gone into the house. Was it over? Had his father finally stopped being mad at him?

He took care of the dishes, wiped down the kitchen, even swept the deck and closed the barbecue. But when all the jobs he could think of had been done, only half an hour had passed. He wandered around the house, flipped through some channels on the television, tried a couple of games on the Internet, thought vaguely of calling Riley, but couldn't settle on anything.

As he passed his brother's closed door Alex heard a strange sound and paused. When had Mark returned home? He heard it again, a tortured, brutal sound. Alex tapped softly on the door then pushed it open. Mark knelt at the side of his bed, arms flung across the covers, sobbing. The horrible sound wrenched at Alex and he quickly, silently shut the door.

Alex didn't know what to do. He took several deep breaths, and then walked slowly outside again. Determined to stay out of the house, he looked around, seeking something to do, and then he remembered noticing some creaking boards in the tree house. Relieved to have thought of a job, he found the tools he needed and headed out to the old maple.

On his hands and knees, Alex moved around the small space, stopping when he heard a creak. He hammered each guilty board silent with far more force than was necessary, using more nails than he needed, but he was unable to stop. If he stopped he'd have to think about why his little brother was crying.

At last, exhausted and out of nails, he hung his head, and it was then that he noticed a blackened spot on the floorboards. Memory washed through him as he ran his fingers across the charred wood.

All they'd wanted was a campfire so they could roast marshmallows. What Alex and Mark had ended up with was a smoke-filled tree house and very, very angry parents. Alex smiled at the memory of their smoke-streaked faces staring at each other in horror as their father raced across the yard.

He brushed the dirt from his fingers and crawled forward to dangle his legs over the edge. There was still enough light in the sky that he could look out over the back of their property, could just make out the fence that ran between them and their neighbour. They'd had a good time living here as kids, tons of open space to explore, a creek running across the back corner.

He was so lost in thought that he didn't hear Mark until his brother's head appeared at the top of the ladder. Startled, Alex looked down into Mark's red-rimmed eyes. The skin of his brother's face was swollen, the grey of his hoodie making his pallor even more gruesome. No way Mark would come here, face his brother, unless he had something to say. Alex looked away, his heart beating like crazy as Mark climbed through the hole in the floor and dropped down beside him, blocking the only exit.

An owl flew past overhead.

"You remember when we would sleep out here?" Alex asked, determined to fill the silence, to keep things from being said that could never be *un*said. "Remember how freaked we were any time an owl or a bat flew past? Or that time a raccoon got into the garbage bins and scared the crap out of us? I didn't think you'd ever stop screaming, Markie." He slapped his leg and forced out a loud, grating laugh.

"I'm gay," Mark said. Just like that, he said it. But Alex ploughed ahead. He didn't know what else to do.

"Or how 'bout the time we decided we wanted a rope swing," Alex went on. "Remember? We got all that rope and stole a tire from Mr. Soo's garage. Nearly broke our friggin' necks trying to hook that up. Good thing Dad found us before we actually tried swinging on the damn thing, or we might have killed ourselves." His voice trailed off in false laughter, and then they were just sitting there together in miserable silence. Mark took a deep breath.

"I talked to one of the counsellors at school. He said I should choose someone to tell. He said it was too big a burden to carry alone."

"I don't know if I can ... I should go," Alex said.

"Please, Alex!" Mark cried, grabbing Alex's arm, shaking him. "I need you to listen to me! If I don't tell someone ..."

"Tell someone else!" Alex wrenched his arm

free, rubbing at the bare skin as he begged Mark with his eyes.

"There isn't anyone else to tell! Please don't be this way, man. I really need you. You're my brother, Alex. I can't tell Mom or Dad. I can't tell Father Birch. You're the only one I can tell and if you brush me off, I'm dead. I really am."

He was crying, his face turned away. Alex wanted to jump to his feet and run as far and as fast as he could possibly go, to a place where this hadn't happened, where his little brother hadn't just confirmed the suspicions and doubts Alex had been harbouring for days now. No, longer than that.

"Alex?" Mark said softly. "Come on, man, I'm the same person I was at dinner. You just know more about me now."

"I don't want to know this about you!" Alex cried.

"*Neither do I!*" Mark exploded.

"Then don't! Go find yourself a girl and *try* for God's sake," Alex shouted right back. "How can you even know you don't like girls when you've never even been with one?"

"How do you know I've never been with a girl?" Mark asked. "You think you're some kind of expert 'cause you've copped a feel a couple of times?"

Alex opened his mouth to speak but Mark was quicker, angrier. Words poured out of him. "Must be nice to be able to squeeze her ass, slip your hand up under her shirt, cop a feel, stuff your tongue down her throat whenever you feel like it. You slept with her yet? I bet a —"

Alex was on him before he even realized what he was doing. They toppled over, the floor of the tree house groaning under their combined weight.

"Shut your bloody face!" he screamed, his fist raised.

"Or what?" Mark demanded, lying panting beneath Alex. "Go ahead and hit me. See if you can pound it out of me, Alex. See if it works. God knows it's never worked for me."

Alex sat back on his haunches and stared at his brother. He realized he didn't know this person, this angry, frustrated kid with the dark, hurting eyes pinned beneath him. He shoved at his brother, hard, and made his way down the ladder into the dark yard.

Chapter 10

Mark was alone in the kitchen when Alex stumbled in Friday morning, yawning and rubbing his eyes. He had not had a good night, but, he realized, glancing at his brother's dark-circled eyes, neither had Mark. He grabbed dishes from the cupboard and sat at the table.

"Mom and Dad gone already?" he asked, pouring milk into a bowl.

"Yeah, left about a half hour ago," Mark told him, shovelling cereal into his mouth while he looked at the paper.

"Pass the milk?" Alex asked. He held out his hand for the ceramic jug. Mark handed it over.

His brother looked exactly the way he had the night before: dark, shaggy hair hanging in his face, pale skin, shoulders slumped, dressed head to toe in black. He was his usual charming, talkative self, too. But, now, every time Alex looked at his brother across the breakfast table, all he saw was someone who was gay.

"It's not catching you know," Mark said.

"Never said it was." Alex looked down at the section of newspaper spread out in front of him.

Mark put the spoon down in his empty cereal bowl. "You gonna be a jerk about this, now?" he asked, leaning forward in his chair.

"I'm not being a jerk."

His brother snorted. Alex pushed his chair away from the table, the legs scraping against the tile floor.

"What the hell do you want from me?" he demanded, anger surging through him. "You want me to pat you on the back and tell you it's okay you're gay? That it doesn't change anything?"

"That'd be good, yeah," Mark said.

"Well I can't. It does change —"

"No it —"

"Don't try to tell me that your life is the same as it was before you figured this out about yourself, 'cause I don't believe it!" Alex cried. "How long did you fight knowing this? A day? A month? A year?" He paused, breathing heavily, but Mark didn't answer him. "Exactly," Alex continued. "But I'm supposed to be good with it after twelve hours?"

Alex shot his brother one last look then stormed out of the kitchen, taking refuge in his room. He threw himself down on his unmade bed and stared up at the ceiling. He *hated* knowing this secret about Mark, hated looking at a guy he'd lived with his whole life and seeing a stranger.

How many other people he'd grown up with had secrets like this? How did *their* families cope with the information? Alex doubted he was the only one struggling. He heard the front door open and slam shut, the sound of his brother's sneakers on the boards of the verandah then crunching down the gravel driveway until it was quiet again. Alex let out a big breath, and closed his eyes.

***

Alex left work that night after helping to lock up. He said goodbye to his co-worker and made his way to the back corner of the parking lot where he'd left his car. Rolling down the windows to find any random gust of cool air, he leaned his head back and just sat, letting himself unwind.

He rubbed his neck. Would this new information about his brother ever get easier to know? Sighing, he reached for his seatbelt wanting, suddenly, to be at home. As he put the keys in the ignition he heard something over near the fence. Alex peered into the dimness, the only light coming from the parking lot lights.

He heard the sound again and recognized human voices, what sounded like several of them, raised in anger. The hair went up on the back of his neck. His first instinct was just to get the hell out of there. He didn't need to find himself at the wrong end of someone else's battle. He was about to start the engine when there was more yelling.

"Screw off!" one of the voices said clearly. This voice was choked with fear but it was undeniably Mark's.

Alex pulled the keys out again and climbed from the car. He wasn't at all sure what he was going to do or say as he moved slowly toward the voices.

"I said back off. Leave us alone," another voice said.

"Or what?" a strange voice said. "What are you and your little boyfriend gonna do?"

Alex took a deep breath and let it out. He grabbed a good-sized branch from the ground and held it at his side. The further he moved from the parking lot the darker it became but slowly his eyes adjusted to the dim light. Then he saw them. What light there was came from behind Alex, illuminating the three attackers who were closing in on Mark and his friend; it was too dark to see who he was with but Alex guessed it might be Scott. Alex swallowed hard, taking his time, realizing he had no clear idea what he was going to do.

"Why don't you run, see how far you get before we catch you?" another voice said.

Alex stifled a gasp, recognizing Kyle Jeffries' voice. His heart sank but he forced himself to keep walking. There were three of them, two guys Alex didn't recognize and Kyle, his short, blonde hair sticking out from under his baseball cap in tufts.

He took a breath then stepped forward.

"Hey, Jeffries," Alex called out. "I thought I recognized your voice."

Alex couldn't control the shaking in his hands, in his legs, couldn't control his racing heart. He held the stick tightly in his right hand, but kept it behind him, out of sight. Mark looked up, frowning, but Alex kept his focus on Kyle.

"Straker?" Kyle squinted at Alex in the poor light. Did Kyle Jeffries know Mark was Alex's brother? Alex couldn't remember if they'd ever met. Kyle didn't go to their high school and Mark never went to Alex's games …

"How's it going?" Alex asked, forcing a calmness he didn't feel. He shot a pointed look at his brother and Scott.

"I'm good," Kyle began, but Mark and Scott had taken the hint and were walking toward the parking lot.

"Go ahead," one of the guys called after them. "We'll catch up with you some other time."

"We better go too," said Kyle with a dark expression. "See you later, Straker."

Alex watched them walk off in the other direction, and then they were gone. He dropped the stick, and jogged after his brother.

"What happened?" he asked when he reached the two boys.

"They followed us out of Tim Horton's, 'round the corner," Scott told him. He kept shooting glances at Mark, who still had not said anything.

He stood, hands shoved deep in the pockets of his jeans, dark eyes watching Alex.

Alex focused his attention on Scott. His brother's friend was several inches taller than Mark and he was stockier. Scott could have taken any of Kyle's punk friends on easily. But Mark ...

"You guys hurt?" Alex asked.

"Naw, they didn't touch us," Scott answered. "Just threatened. Thanks for bailing us out — don't think we could have outrun them."

"Come on," Alex told them, heading for the car. He was almost there when he realized he wasn't being followed. Turning he saw his brother standing in the same spot. Scott stood beside Mark looking helplessly from Mark to Alex.

"Are you coming?" Alex asked. "I'll take you home."

"We're good," Mark said, his voice still rough with fear.

"What do you mean 'we're good'?" Alex asked. "You nearly —"

"Some friends you have, Alex," his brother interrupted. "Why didn't you tell them that I'm your brother?"

"I just wanted to get you guys out of there," Alex tried to explain. "I didn't think Kyle needed to know anything more about you."

"Yeah, that was it," Mark said sarcastically. "You were thinking of me and Scott."

"Mark, just leave it," Scott said, looking from one brother to the other. "Alex did save our asses

80

just now."

"What are you saying, Mark?" Alex asked, as though Scott hadn't spoken at all.

"Having a gay brother doesn't fit with your jock *persona*, does it Alex?" Mark said, his voice cold, hard. "Come on Scott, let's go." He turned his back on Alex.

"You're kidding me," Alex said, frowning. "What if those jerks come back? Just let me take you home, Mark. Don't be an idiot."

"Thanks for bailing us out, Alex," Scott said at last, running a hand through his short, dark curls. "We owe ya one, man. But we'll grab the bus."

Helplessly Alex watched the two of them walk toward the bus stop. He almost ran after them, prepared to haul his brother back to the car, force him into it. Instead he drove home and lay in bed, fully alert, until he heard the front door open and close and his brother's footsteps going into his own room. Only then did he relax.

Alex was just about asleep when he heard a sound coming from Mark's room. He held still, listening. And then he heard it again.

"Help me, Lord, please help me," his brother's tortured voice said. "Help me, Lord, please help me. Help me, Lord, please help me."

Chapter 11

"What have you got planned for tonight, Alex?" Mr. Straker asked on Saturday evening, lifting his car keys from the hook by the door.

"Laura's coming over, we're going to watch a movie," Alex said, wishing his parents would just hurry up and *leave*.

"Well, have a nice evening, Alex," his mother told him with a smile and a small wink.

"Yeah, you too."

"Oh, I'm sure Marnie will have gone to way too much trouble. She always does," Mrs. Straker said, shaking her head. She slipped her handbag over one shoulder and followed her husband to the front door. "You'd think with five kids she'd be busy enough."

Alex closed the door on the rest of his mother's sentence, not wanting to hear about Marnie Carruthers. He thought instead of Laura, on her way over this very minute, of having the house to themselves for the entire evening. What Alex wanted more than anything was to just cuddle with Laura on the couch, to touch her, to smell her. He didn't want to think about or talk about anything. He just wanted to *be*.

Ten minutes later, Laura was already waving a bag of chips at him as she walked through the door. "I brought snacks!" she announced. "And dip!"

"You sure you don't want a nice healthy veggie platter?"

"Screw healthy," Laura replied, tossing him the bag.

They found something to drink and took their loot into the family room. Alex picked up the remote, turning to Laura.

"Ready?" he asked.

"Nope," Laura told him with a quick shake of her head. "I want to see the rest of the house. Take me on a tour."

"Really? Why?"

"You're such a guy, Alex," Laura told him, grabbing his arm and marching him down the hall.

"I thought that was what you liked about me."

"Oooh, you made a joke! Did it hurt?"

"Only a little. Okay, this is —"

"No! Don't tell me. I want to guess." Laura pushed open the door and stepped over the threshold. She looked around slowly and a smile crept over her face.

"This is definitely not *your* room," she announced. "Not a single trophy, ribbon, award, certificate. Plus, way too many books," she teased, kissing his cheek.

Mark's room *was* pretty bare; the bookcase was jammed full of books, the single bed was neatly made. There was a dresser, and a desk with a computer sitting on it. The only thing on the walls was a crucifix above the bed. A mental image popped into his head of his brother, arms splayed across the mattress, sobbing, and praying desperately for help, and Alex hustled Laura out of the room.

"Now this screams Alexander Straker," she affirmed when he opened the door to his own room.

"Screams?"

"Oh completely. I mean, what will you do when these shelves are full? Take out the ceiling?"

"Naw, we're going to convert the spare room," he told her, leading her down the hall.

He quickly showed her his parents' room, the guest room, and the bathroom (why she needed to see *that* he had no clue) and then dragged her back to the family room.

"I love your house, Alex," Laura said with a wistful sigh. "It's so cozy and warm, all the rich colours and textures. Your parents did a great job."

"My parents?" Alex scoffed. "My mom did it all. Dad doesn't decorate. He builds."

"Really? Oh. Well, some guys do. My dad did

a lot of the work with Mom in our old house."

"You miss it, don't you?" he asked, watching her run her fingers over the pillows and blanket on the couch. He'd never been concerned about his home before, or how it looked. It was just a place to eat, sleep, and get yelled at occasionally. But for Laura it was so much more than that.

"Yeah, a lot," she said, a catch in her voice. "I had the most amazing bedroom. My mom had painted a mural along one wall. She stencilled lines from one of my favourite books along the top of the wall as a border," she said, describing it to him until Alex could see the English countryside, could smell the flowers and hear the birds. She turned back to him, smiling, though her eyes were damp. "I hated leaving my room, that house. All those memories …"

Laura cleared her throat, then she drifted over to the built-in bookcase by the fireplace and glanced over the shelves of books and family photos.

"Oh, this is a nice photo," she said, picking up a framed picture. She giggled. "How old were you when this was taken?" she asked, crossing the room to show him.

Alex barely glanced at it. "Thirteen, I think," he said vaguely. He sat on the couch, hoping she'd get the hint.

"And look at Mark! Oh my God, he's so *short*!" She laughed again. "And Emma had braces. Wow," Laura said, setting the photograph back on the shelf. "You guys must have done tons together as families, eh?"

"Yeah, I guess." He eyed the DVD case lying on the ottoman but Laura was determined to reminisce.

"Did you know that Emma used to have the biggest crush on you?"

Alex blushed. "Yeah, I knew," he said. "Then she met Riley and never looked at me again."

"Well, things always have a way of working out for the best, don't they?" Laura told him with a smile, joining him on the couch. She nestled the chip bowl and the container of dip in her lap and Alex pressed play.

They watched for a while but he couldn't concentrate on the story; the characters were silly stereotypes, the dialogue lame. Laura was pressed up against him. Alex adjusted his arm around her and she settled into him, the bare skin of her arm smooth beneath his hand as he stroked it. The tiny blonde hairs stood up for him, goosebumps formed and Alex grinned.

He leaned over and kissed her head. She turned her face to him and he kissed her lips, then down her cheek, across the skin on her neck. Slowly, gently he eased her back on the couch then lowered himself so they were stretched out side by side. Propping himself up on one elbow Alex gazed at her.

"What are you looking at?" Laura asked.

"You. Geez you're gorgeous," he whispered,

then kissed the faint pink that sprang up in her neck.

This was the way it was *meant* to be: all this amazing, soft skin, silky hair, full, lush lips seeking out his. He couldn't get enough of her, couldn't touch enough of her at one time. And no matter how much he touched her, kissed her, the pressure never eased off, it grew stronger. She put her arms around his neck and kissed him. Her fingers fluttered gently across his back and then she pressed him against her.

Alex couldn't catch a solid breath; he felt as though he was going to explode. He ground himself against her, not caring, not caring at all. The only thing he could think of was getting rid of the terrible pressure that kept building and building. It would kill him, he was sure. This was so *right*, so *true*, being here with this beautiful, amazing girl. Nothing else was as real as this.

"Alex," her strangled voice came to him, calling over the crashing waves. "Alex!"

He struggled to the surface, and all at once he was on the floor, the family room carpet rough against the skin of his back. Laura had pushed him off her! He sat up. Laura was sitting up on the couch, her eyes wide, as she struggled to straighten her T-shirt, adjust her bra.

Alarmed, *terrified*, Alex got to his feet. "Laura, I'm sorry," he began, but she held out a hand stopping him.

"It's okay," she assured him, her voice shaky.

"We both got a little carried away."

She ran her hands over her head, gathered her hair together then let it fall in a sheet down her back. She did it again and then once more, her breathing slowly returning to normal. As Alex watched her, he felt his own pulse slow, his blood stop pounding through him. He ran a hand across his forehead, rubbed his eyes.

"Oh, it's late," Laura said, glancing at the clock over the fireplace. "I should probably go home anyway."

"You don't have to leave," Alex told her. "I promise to behave myself."

Laura laughed. "What if *I* can't behave? I'll see you tomorrow, okay?"

Guilt must have still been all over his face because Laura reached out and touched his cheek, kissing him once, quickly.

"It's okay, Alex."

He walked her out to her car, watched her drive away, then went back inside and had a very long, very cold shower.

Chapter 12

Music pounded from the speakers aimed out the windows of the house and kids filled the basement and the yard. The large cement patio had turned into a dance floor and several couples were pressed up against each other, barely moving. Laura and Alex shared a lawn chair and a beer, taking turns sipping from the ice-cold can.

"You think Jenny has any idea how many people are here?" Laura asked.

"Better for her if she doesn't," Alex replied. He set the empty beer can down and wrapped his arms around Laura.

"Dance with me," she breathed into his ear, the strong smell of yeast wafting over him. She pulled on his hand.

"I'm not that great a dancer," Alex said.

"That's okay, neither am I. Come on, please?"

Alex slid off the lawn chair and allowed

himself to be led. Laura wrapped her arms around his neck and Alex slid his own around her waist. She rested her head against his chest and they swayed together. He closed his eyes, making it easier to imagine they were alone. He could feel the heat of her from the press of her hair against his chest all the way down to her thighs. The music pulsed in his head and the blood pulsed in his veins. He took a deep breath and let it out slowly. Tonight he was staying in control.

Laura looked up at him and smiled. "This is very nice," she said. "I thought you were a bad dancer."

"I never said I was a bad dancer. I just said I wasn't a *great* dancer," he reminded her.

"Whatever. Other than Wii Tennis, is there anything you aren't good at?"

She tilted her head so her face was right there, her eyes bright, her mouth teasing him. He kissed her lightly and pulled back but her hand on the back of his head brought their mouths together again, harder.

"Get a room," someone said, dancing past. Alex pulled away from Laura, embarrassment flooding him.

"Oh whatever, Garrett," Laura said, laughing. "Don't listen to him, Alex. He's just jealous."

"Of me?" Alex asked, the thought giving him a little surge of pride.

Laura laughed and swatted him playfully on the arm. "No, silly, of *me!*" She frowned. "You know

Garrett's gay, right?" she asked.

Alex was stunned. *Garrett? Gay?*

"You really didn't know that?" Laura said, drawing his attention back to her, searching his face.

"No," he said. "I guess I wasn't around when it was announced."

"Oh yeah? When did you announce you were straight?" Laura scowled at him, suddenly wary. "You don't have a problem with this, right? He's the same guy you knew half an hour ago."

Now where had he heard that line before? Alex scanned the party for Garrett and found him standing with some other guys on the lawn. If Laura hadn't told him the guy was gay, Alex would never have guessed. There was nothing that set him apart from the others.

But now that he did know, Alex looked at Garrett differently. Just like people would look at Mark when they found out. Just like *Alex* looked at Mark now that he knew.

Eventually they drifted off the dance floor. Alex helped himself to another beer.

"You want another?" he asked Laura, but she shook her head.

"One's enough for me," she told him.

Alex sat down in a big easy chair in the family room and Laura perched on his lap. Riley and Emma joined them, then a few others, including Garrett. The group started talking about their courses for fall but Alex couldn't focus on the conversation.

He'd felt slightly less wretched the last few days but now, armed with new surprises and more beer than he usually drank, he was feeling like crap again. No one was who he or she appeared to be. How many of these people gathered here were keeping secrets? How many others at school, at his church? First Paul Carruthers, then Mark, now Garrett. Who was Laura, really? He sipped at his beer, keeping his eyes on the rug at his feet.

"Hey, Garrett," one of the girls called. "You see that story in the paper the other day about the attack on Davie Street?"

Garrett's open, smiling face darkened. "Yeah. Cowards," he muttered.

"Well, the victims were holding hands," Fletcher said. "I mean, come on, if you're going to *flaunt* it —"

"Since when is holding hands flaunting anything?" Laura demanded, shifting on Alex's legs. "You hold hands with Elyse in public all the time. Hell you've done a lot more than hold her hand …"

"I'm not gay."

Exactly, Alex thought.

"Don't ask, don't tell — is that what you're saying, Fletcher?" Garrett said at last. "Sorry, I'm not going to hide who I am just to make everyone else feel better. If I want to hold my boyfriend's hand walking down the street, then why shouldn't I? Why is it so different when I do it?"

Alex took a long swallow of his beer, draining the can. Wasn't it easier to just blend in? At least appear to be like everyone else? Those guys who got beat up on Davie Street wouldn't have attracted as much attention if they'd just tried to blend in.

"When my cousin came out last year, my uncle blew a fuse," Riley said, joining the conversation. "Scott said to him, 'I thought you just wanted me to be happy, Dad. Or was that only if I was a *het-ero*sexual.' But what do you expect? The old guy was raised to believe gays are sinners."

"Excuse me," Alex said, almost dumping Laura on the floor in his hurry to get away. He fled to the small kitchen at the back of the room, his heart pounding. He grabbed another beer from the ice chest on the floor, opened it, and drank it without stopping. Riley's cousin was Scott, Mark's *friend*. What if Mark was just confused and Scott had talked him into it? What if it was all Scott's fault?

"Hey, Alex." Garrett grabbed a bag of chips off the counter and ripped it open. "You having a good summer?" he asked, tossing a handful into his mouth.

Alex struggled to keep his balance. All of a sudden his head felt like it wasn't attached properly to his neck. "I'm good, yeah. You?" he muttered.

"Can't complain," Garrett said easily. "Well, I could, but it doesn't get us anywhere, does it? Excuse me," he said, leaning across Alex to grab a beer from the cooler. As he walked back to the group Alex followed him.

"Do you guys have a code?" he asked.

"Excuse me?"

"Do ... you ... have ... a code," Alex repeated, slowly. "Gay guys, I mean."

"Alex!" Laura cried, grabbing his arm. He shook her off.

"No, no code," Garrett said, taking a step toward his seat.

"How do you know who's who? I mean, you don't want to be asking a straight guy out on a date," Alex continued. "That could get tricky."

All conversation stopped, leaving a very awkward silence.

"Hey, man," Garrett said with an uneasy laugh. "I think you've had too much to drink."

"Alex, what are you doing?" Laura grabbed his arm again and pulled hard.

"I'm just asking Garrett here how he can tell which guys are gay ..."

"I think it's time to go home, Alex," Riley said, appearing beside him and gripping Alex's elbow tightly.

Chapter 13

"You want some help getting him home, Laura?" Riley asked as they left the house and headed for Alex's car.

"No, thanks," Laura told him. "I'll be okay."

"Well, call me if you need me," Riley told her, and headed back to the party.

Laura drove in silence, her eyes on the road. Alex watched her, could see the tension in her neck and shoulders. "Look," he said at last, "I know I was a bit of a jerk back there, but —"

"A bit of a jerk?" Laura cried. "What were you thinking?"

"I wasn't thinking," he confessed. "I shouldn't have had so much to drink."

"No, really? Do you have any idea how embarrassing that was? And what about Garrett?" She swerved into an empty parking lot and stopped the car, turning to glare directly at Alex. "How could you say those things to him, in front of our friends, *Garrett's* friends? Do you have any idea how hard it was for him to come out in the first place? How much he has to deal with? The one place, the *one* place he can relax," she repeated, poking Alex in the chest, "where he feels safe, is with his friends. And you embarrass him!"

Suddenly Laura ran out of words. She stuffed her hands between her knees and bent her head. Alex looked at her, taking in the fall of hair as it shielded her face, the hunched shoulders. He had done this. He had made Laura hate him. And yet he still couldn't find the words to make it right.

"Laura, I'm sorry. I'll apologize to Garrett …"

"Is it a Catholic thing?" she demanded.

"Is what a Catholic thing?"

"Your homophobia."

Alex flinched. "I'm not homophobic," he began but Laura's unpleasant laugh stopped him.

"No?" she said. "Really. As soon as I told you Garrett was gay your whole attitude changed. I could feel you tense up. And then you start asking Garrett really ignorant, *stupid* questions."

"I *know*! I said I was sorry!" What did she want from him? What were the right words?

"I shouldn't be surprised, really," Laura continued as though Alex hadn't spoken at all. "I know the church doesn't think too much of homosexuality. If you grow up being told that something's wrong …"

"I wasn't brought up being told homosexuality

96

was wrong," Alex interrupted. He may not attend the church anymore but for some reason he still felt protective of it. Of his parents. "We never *talked* about it at all. I …"

"So maybe it's just *this* Catholic who has a problem with gays."

Alex pressed his hands into his eyes until it hurt. Was he homophobic? It wasn't something he'd ever stopped to think about. Until Mark, until Garrett, Alex hadn't known anyone who was gay. Was he struggling to accept Mark's announcement because he thought being gay was wrong? No, he didn't believe that. Did he? His temples throbbed and he longed for his bed, for sleep.

"You want to tell me what's going on, Alex?" Laura asked at last.

"Going on?" Alex said, confused by the sudden change of direction the conversation had just taken.

"You've been edgy and distracted for days. You obviously aren't sleeping very well 'cause you look like crap. Then tonight you start drinking and acting stupid. It's obvious that something's bothering you."

"I apologized for that," Alex said helplessly.

"Why won't you just *talk* to me?" Laura cried, her anger filling the space between them. "You don't ever share anything with me. Oh, other than your spit."

Heat filled Alex's neck and face. He stared at his hands, folded in his lap. "I don't know what you mean," he muttered. "We talk all the time."

"Do we? Really. What do we talk about?"

"I don't know, the weather, sports, what movies we like," he scrambled. "I thought we were having a good time."

"We do have fun together!" Laura cried, her eyes bright with tears. "But you never share anything with me! Not your feelings, not your ideas or thoughts about stuff. Any time I ask, you shut me down! Or tell me nothing's wrong when it's totally obvious something is. Why won't you talk to me?"

"It's not my secret to share!" Alex cried, wrenching at the door handle, desperate to escape. His car had never seemed so small, so tomb-like. He paced the deserted parking lot, breathing the night air deeply into his lungs.

Laura climbed out of the car after him and leaned against the door. He could feel her eyes on him. Gradually he slowed his frantic pacing although he couldn't stay still, had to keep moving. The secret was a stone inside him, weighing him down.

"I'm sorry, Alex," Laura began, "You don't have to betray anyone's secret ..."

"No! No," he repeated. "I can't do it anymore. I don't *want* to know this by myself anymore." He looked at her, standing quietly in the moonlight. "It's Mark. He's gay. He told me last week."

He stopped pacing and leaned against a stone wall, out of words and energy. But despite his overwhelming fatigue and the heaviness of the air, Alex felt lighter than he had in days.

"That's a pretty big secret," Laura said softly.

Alex looked at her, nodded. "I think I knew before he told me," he went on, the words coming more easily now that he'd begun. "I saw him with, with Scott, they were hugging ..."

"He has a boyfriend?" Laura asked.

"Yeah, I guess," Alex admitted, flinching at the term. "I said I'd seen him hug the guy. He brushed it off, but I think I knew then. He's been so miserable this summer. I've heard him crying in his room, praying ..." He closed his eyes. What response did Mark hope he would get to his prayers? What answer was there?

Laura joined him and wrapped her arms around his waist. "I think I knew too," she said against his shirt. "In the music store that time, remember? There was something about the way he looked at the guy he was with — I guess it was Scott. It was the same look you give me sometimes."

He didn't want to *know* this! He didn't want to imagine his brother with a *guy* doing the things he and Laura did. *So don't. It's none of your business, anyway.*

"It must have been such a relief for him to tell someone," Laura said.

"I guess, maybe," Alex said, thinking of Mark refusing to accept a ride home from his own brother. Did Mark regret sharing his secret with him? Alex pushed away from the wall and headed toward the car.

"I know this has been really hard for you to hear, Alex," Laura said, slipping her hand into his. "But it'll get easier. He's still your brother. And look at it this way," she went on, nudging him, "you won't ever have to compete for girls —"

Chapter 14

"Will you take these out to the van, Alex?" Mrs. Straker asked, handing him several metal cookie tins. "I want to get them to Marnie. They're for the lunch Sunday."

"Yeah, sure," he mumbled, heading outside. He'd forgotten about the baptism and party. His stomach lurched. How long was he going to have to keep *that* secret? It had been a huge relief to tell Laura about Mark but there was no way he was telling her about Paul Carruthers.

He was putting the cookie tins on the passenger seat when his mother came out carrying two bags. "You trying to feed an army?" he asked. His mother shot him a look as she added her bags to the tins and closed the door.

"What's with the attitude?" she asked, going around the car and climbing behind the wheel. "You have a problem with me helping my friend?"

"No, sorry," he said blushing.

"I'll be back in a few hours," she told him, pulling the door closed.

Alex backed away as his mother turned the key in the ignition. The engine sputtered but didn't turn over. She tried again, still nothing. Through the Odyssey's window Alex could see his mom muttering to herself as she tried unsuccessfully to get the van to start. Finally she opened the door and climbed out.

"I let your father borrow my van one time and he brings it back broken," she said, her eyes flashing.

Alex stifled a laugh. "I can give you a ride, Mom," he offered. "I'm heading into town anyway."

Ten minutes later they were in the Corolla, his mother's anger gone as quickly as it had come. She rolled down her window and let what breeze there was in the car.

"It looks as though the weather will be good Sunday," she said. "Paul and Marnie will be able to have everyone outside."

"That's nice," Alex said, coming to a stop at a light.

"Well, it's less stress for Marnie, not having to handle so many guests inside," she went on. "She's been so busy lately! One or another of the little ones has been sick, Paul's been away from home more than usual …"

The second the light went green Alex hit the

gas, shooting them into the intersection. His mother grabbed the dashboard. "Careful!" she cried.

"Sorry, Mom. You okay?"

"I'm fine," she said, glancing at him.

He was careful to drive as though he were taking his road test, eyes never leaving the road, though his heart continued to pound.

"Laura told me she plans to come with us on Sunday," Mrs. Straker said. "I'm glad she's exploring, asking questions. No one encouraged me to do that when I was your age and struggling with who I was and why I was here."

Alex shifted in his seat, cleared his throat. Where was this leading? He hadn't offered her a ride just so he could be trapped into hearing a lecture.

"Then I met your dad," his mom went on. "I was so crazy about him I started going to church just to have that extra hour with him!" She giggled and Alex grinned despite himself, picturing a much younger Joanna trailing after her boyfriend into church.

"Then gradually I realized I was going because I wanted to," she said. "Faith is a very, very personal thing, Alex. And no one promised it would be a smooth road."

Alex pulled into the Carruthers' driveway and turned off the car, then sat staring at the front of the house. His mom reached out her hand and touched his cheek gently.

"I know your dad has been leaning on you pretty hard about your decision," she said softly. "He's never had a moment's doubt about his faith …"

"Lucky him," Alex muttered, pulling away from her hand. He climbed quickly out of the car and headed to the trunk, flinging it open.

He unloaded her packages as she went to the front door, knocking once before opening it and stepping in. In a second Mrs. Carruthers appeared on the doorstep.

"Thanks for helping Joanna get here, Alex!" she said, taking one of the bags from him. She smiled but Alex noticed the dark circles under her eyes. "I don't know what I'd do without her."

"No problem," he said. "You okay getting home, Mom?" he asked, anxious to get away.

"Oh I'm fine," Mrs. Straker said. "If nothing else your father can come and get me since it's his fault my van won't start! Thanks for the ride, Alex."

"I'll see you later."

Climbing into the car he glanced up at the house. His mother had slipped an arm around Mrs. Carruthers' shoulders and almost seemed to be supporting her as they went inside and shut the door.

She knows something's going on with her husband. He backed out of the driveway and headed for Laura's.

***

Alex held on tightly to Laura's hand as they

walked toward the large wooden doors of the church. The couples and families streaming in were people Alex had known his whole life. They smiled at him, nodding. A few people said good morning just as they had every Sunday.

Inside the vestibule, everything looked so familiar: the statue of Mary holding an infant Jesus, the hand woven tapestry hanging behind her, the bulletin board with notices for church fundraisers and meetings layered on its surface. There was old Mrs. Alvarez selling tickets to something.

"Good morning, Alex." Father Birch stood in front of him, holding out his hand.

Alex shook it. "Good morning, Father," he managed to say with only a slight tremor in his voice. He introduced Laura and took a step to leave.

"It's good to see you again," the priest went on pleasantly. "It's been a while."

Alex wished the floor would open up and swallow him. He concentrated on a spot slightly to the left of the priest's ear. "Yeah, well ..."

Father Birch leaned in ever so slightly and lowered his voice. "You know you can come and talk to me anytime, Alex. Maybe I can help," he said, then he moved off to speak to someone else.

"Relax, would you?" Laura whispered, giving his hand a shake as he pulled her forward.

"I'm relaxed ..."

"Really?" she said. "Then why are my fingers

being crushed?"

"Sorry," Alex muttered, loosening his grip. *You can do this*, he told himself, letting out a breath.

They passed a cluster of young altar servers, their sneakers peeking out from beneath the bottoms of their robes.

"Were you an altar server?" Laura asked.

"Yeah, for a few years."

"I bet you were awfully cute in your long red robe, blonde hair sticking up at the back of your head," she teased.

"Mostly I was nervous," he confessed, remembering. "All those eyes watching. Mark kept making faces at me, trying to get me to laugh," he said. "I did the same to him a year later, when he started serving."

Alex found where his family was sitting and he and Laura slid in beside them. He sank onto the hard wooden pew, grateful for the silence. Laura pulled out the small book Mark had given her that explained the Mass and began to read. On her other side Mark was still on the padded kneeler, his bowed head resting on his folded hands, his eyes tightly closed.

What did Mark hope would come of his praying? Was there a way to reconcile his brother's strong faith with the way the church felt about gays? If Alex was struggling with his belief in God, how much harder must it be for Mark?

Alex closed his eyes and began, tentatively, to recite the Lord's Prayer, the words as familiar to him as his name. "Our Father, who art in heaven ..." *Are You? If You are really up there, why can't I feel You anymore? How can I know for sure that You are there? What if we're all making a mistake doing this church thing every Sunday?*

The sudden chiming of bells at the back of the church startled Alex out of his thoughts. He stood up beside Laura as the choir began singing the entrance hymn, the familiar words and music filling the church. As the procession made its way up the centre aisle, Alex glanced around. Filling the old wooden pews were all the families he'd known his whole life. Mr. and Mrs. Castillo with their three daughters — Alex had had such a crush on the eldest, Jessica. And over there was old Mrs. Chin with her lace head covering. She always had candies in her coat pocket. And there, on the far side of the church, five children arranged on either side of him and his wife, was Paul Carruthers.

Chapter 15

Alex swallowed hard, closed his eyes and opened them again, rubbed his damp palms down the legs of his tan trousers. He had forgotten, in all his anxiety about returning to church, that *he* would be here this morning. Alex looked over again, easily finding the family in their usual spot: second pew from the front.

Mr. Carruthers stood beside his wife, sharing a hymn book. From where he was standing Alex could only see the back of the man's balding head, the collar of his shirt poking out above his jacket. Mrs. Carruthers leaned in to say something to him then he reached out his hands, accepting the baby from her. He sat down and settled his son on one knee, jiggling him slightly. The baby grabbed at his father's jacket.

Alex felt a tug on his hand. Looking around he saw that everyone was sitting and he sat down beside Laura. She looked at him, her eyes questioning.

"You doing okay?" she asked.

"Yeah. I'm good," he lied, then turned to face the front.

Through the standing and sitting, the kneeling and praying and singing of the next hour Alex sat lost in his thoughts. How could the man just sit there as though nothing were wrong? How could he pretend day after day to be a faithful husband, a faithful Catholic? How many others gathered in the church that morning were living a lie? Is that what being a Christian was all about? Giving the *appearance* of goodness?

"Are you going up, Alex?" Laura asked him.

Alex looked around, frowning. The row of people directly in front of them was filing to the front for communion. He shook his head. "You could go up, though, get a blessing," he said as Mark stood up.

"That's okay," she said, moving her legs to one side to let his family pass. "I'll stay here with you."

Row after row of parishioners shuffled along in the slow moving line. What were they thinking about? Last night's party? Problems with the boss? The girlfriend they were planning to meet later? Alex dropped his eyes to his lap and stared at his clenched hands.

When the Mass was over Father Birch invited the Carruthers family to the front of the church.

Mrs. Carruthers carried Adrian, dressed in a flowing, white baptismal gown, and made her way to the altar. Mr. Carruthers followed her with their four other children and the two godparents.

They gathered, with Father Birch, around the baptismal font. As the priest began to speak Alex felt Laura's hand slip into his. He shifted his position on the bench until he felt the warmth of her skin.

Baby Adrian squawked as the holy water touched his forehead once, twice, then a third time. *I hear you, little guy*, Alex thought. *If I could get away with it, I'd squawk too.*

And then it was over and everyone was filing out, pausing to shake hands with Father Birch, to speak to friends, to congratulate the Carruthers. Alex put a hand on Laura's elbow and guided her out a side door.

"Aren't we going to …"

"We'll see them at the house," Alex said, hurrying her to the car. He helped Laura into the passenger seat then went around to the other side.

"Was it as bad as you thought?" she asked as he buckled his seat belt. "You seemed very far away the whole time."

"It was okay. Familiar, anyway," he admitted.

Laura leaned her head back. "I love how quiet and peaceful it is in church. You can just stop and *be*. I do feel a presence when I'm there. It's very comforting."

What about when you leave? Alex wondered.

Do you feel that presence the rest of the week?

Mrs. Carruthers met them at the front door wearing an apron over her dress and a very bright smile. She accepted Laura's hug and the white wrapped gift, then ushered them through to the yard. "Go on out and join everyone," she told them. "I'm just finishing things up in here. I think Emma and Riley are out there somewhere."

Alex trailed behind Laura into the yard. It was much smaller than the Strakers' and now, crowded with people, it seemed even smaller. Alex spotted his parents sitting under the large elm tree in one corner, the baby on his mother's lap. Paul Carruthers leaned against the table, arms folded across his chest, deep in conversation with Alex's father.

Finally Alex spotted Emma and Riley and led Laura toward them. He kept his back to the yard, his arm around Laura's waist.

"I'm glad you two came," Emma said, hugging Laura. "It's been kind of crazy around here."

"Planning a party can be stressful," Laura agreed.

"Hey, are you guys interested in going camping next week?" Riley asked, handing Alex and Laura glasses of iced tea. "A group of us were thinking of going to Golden Ears for a couple of nights. The weather is supposed to be good and if we go mid-week, we shouldn't have any trouble getting a couple of sites."

Alex and Laura exchanged glances. "I'd have

to rearrange my shifts at work," she said, "but Nikki owes me. What do you think, Alex?"

"Yeah sure, why not? I think we've got a tent somewhere," he said with a grin.

After a while Mrs. Carruthers emerged from the house carrying a tray of sandwiches. Right behind her Emma followed with another tray. People slowly began making their way to the large picnic table set up on the grass. Alex grabbed a plastic plate and loaded it with little triangles of bread. He'd skipped breakfast that morning and was famished.

"Save some for the rest of us, Straker," Riley told him, digging him in the back with the end of a fork.

"Yeah, yeah, there's tons," Alex shot back, reaching for a napkin.

"He always did have a healthy appetite," a voice said. Alex looked up to find Paul Carruthers standing at the end of the table, beer in hand, a jovial grin on his face. "How are things going Alex?" the man asked. "Haven't seen you much this summer."

"Been busy, working," Alex muttered, heat rushing to his face.

Mr. Carruthers laughed loudly and slapped Alex on the shoulder. "That's not all you've been up to," he said. "Emma tells me you have a girl-friend."

I saw you, you fake. I SAW you. The baby carrots on his plate bounced as Alex's hands trembled. He looked up into the man's smiling face, but Alex's face was hard, tight. The words were right there, on the tip of his tongue. Then he felt a strong hand grip his elbow and he was led away. Riley didn't let go of Alex's arm until they'd rounded the corner of the house.

"It's him, isn't it?" he asked.

Alex nodded, staring down at the food on his plate, his appetite completely gone. He didn't bother to deny it or ask how Riley had guessed. "I saw him a few weeks ago."

"You were gonna tell him you knew, right there?!" Riley said, pacing in front of Alex.

"I can't stand knowing this Ri!" Alex cried. "I think Mrs. Carruthers knows or suspects something. She looked pretty rough the other day when I dropped my mom off here."

Riley stopped pacing. "You can't say anything," he said in a tight, low voice. "It'll kill Emma. She adores the jerk."

Alex slumped against the cedar fence, the plate of food still in his hand. He set it down on the grass at his feet. "Maybe if I tell him I know, he'll end it," he said.

"And maybe he won't. Maybe he already has. But it's not our problem, man. It sucks, but you gotta keep it to yourself."

"He just keeps on going to church, letting everyone believe he's a good example of a Christian family man," Alex said as though Riley hadn't spoken at all. "It makes me *sick*!"

"Is that why you stopped going to Mass?" Riley asked. "Because of him?"

Startled, Alex looked up. "Yeah, partly," he admitted.

"That's pretty lame, don't you think? You really gonna give that jerk that much power in your life?"

From the yard came Emma's voice, calling for Riley. With one last, questioning look, Riley disappeared, leaving Alex alone with his thoughts.

Chapter 16

Alex hauled the last of the gear from the back of the van and set it on the ground at his feet. Just across the road a black, bushy-tailed squirrel sat up on his haunches and scolded him. Then it turned and ran as Alex picked up one of the coolers and headed for the picnic table.

"Is that everything?" Laura asked, setting a camp chair down beside the cold fire pit.

"Just the other cooler," he told her, putting the heavy chest down. "But I'll get it. Where'd Riley go?"

"He went off with Matt to get some firewood," Emma told him.

"Did you decide where the tents are going?" he asked.

"Yes," Laura answered. "Girls' tents in this campsite, guys' in that one."

That had been an interesting conversation, Alex

thought, returning to the van for the other cooler. He heard his father's voice in his head, issuing his warnings: "What are the sleeping arrangements going to be on this camping trip? If this outing is just an excuse to misbehave …"

"Maybe you should think about putting up your tent," Laura suggested, breaking into Alex's thoughts. "Or were you guys going to sleep with the bears?"

"What bears? Are there bears around?" Jenny asked, stepping out of a small black hatchback. "No one said anything about bears, Garrett," she said, turning to him as he came around to join her.

"Aw, they're just little black and brown bears, Jen," he teased her. "They aren't nearly as nasty as the grizzlies in Banff."

"I'll get that tent," Alex muttered, pulling the nylon two-man out of its bag. When Riley had told him Garrett was joining the group he'd almost backed out. *Would* have backed out if Laura hadn't threatened to never speak to him again if he didn't just apologize and get over it.

He'd pretty much finished setting the tent up by the time Riley and Matt returned, lugging a leather wood carrier between them. They dropped their load near the fire pit and brushed off their hands. Riley eyed the tent and wiggled the main pole experimentally.

"Is it gonna stay standing, Alex?" Riley asked. "Not gonna fall on us at two in the morning?"

"Just your side, Jacobs," Alex told him, tossing

his sleeping bag and pack into the tent.

"When's Mikaela coming up, Matt?" Emma called. "She is still coming, right?"

"Yeah. Her boss wouldn't let her leave early so she'll drive up when she's done," Matt told her, grabbing a coke from the cooler and dropping into a camp chair. "She said she'd call when she's on her way so we can have a really good fire going."

"Phones don't work up here, Matt," Alex told him. He'd thrown his own cell in the glove box of the van for safekeeping. "We're too far up the mountain."

Matt shrugged. "Guess she's gonna have to take her chances then," he said easily.

"Well, I'm hot," Riley announced, peeling off his T-shirt. "Anyone else for a swim?"

Ten minutes later they were making their way down the trail and over the bridge to the beach. Alex lagged behind, fussing with one arm of his sunglasses. He had just straightened it when he heard pounding footsteps behind him and in another second Garrett was shooting past.

"Hey, Garrett," Alex called. "Wait a sec."

Garrett stopped running and turned to face Alex, a wary look on his face.

"I just wanted to say I'm sorry about the other night at Jenny's. I was out of line," Alex blurted.

For a long second Garrett said nothing, just looked at Alex from beneath the rim of his hat. "You were way out of line," he said at last.

"I know it, man. Look," he adjusted his ball cap

then let out a breath. "I just found out that my kid brother, well, he came out to me a couple of weeks ago." He wasn't sure what he'd expected or hoped by sharing Mark's secret with Garrett.

"And so?"

Okay, so the guy wasn't going to make it easy for Alex. "And so I've been, I'm just kind of ..." he struggled but the words wouldn't come.

He cleared his throat. "Thanks for apologizing," he said, and headed toward the others gathered in the lake.

Alex whipped his cap off his head and ran the back of his hand across his forehead, wiping away the sweat. After a long moment he followed Garrett.

***

The fire, originally a towering inferno thanks to way too much wood, had burned down to a gentle blaze, and darkness had settled in completely around the four couples. Every once in a while a laugh or raised voice drifted on the night air but otherwise the campground had fallen silent. Alex leaned drowsily against Laura, snuggling with her under the sleeping bag.

"I wish we could spend the night together," he whispered.

"Alex," she warned, "we discussed this. We agreed we weren't ready ..."

"Not for *that*," he clarified. "It just feels so good being close to you like this." She was so warm and soft. And she smelled amazing, all smoky. He nuzzled her neck, pulling her close to him.

"Anyone want another s'more?" Mikaela asked, holding out the bag of marshmallows.

"Aw, Mikaela, put those away!" Matt groaned, wrestling the bag from her hands. They tumbled over, wrestling on the fir-needle strewn ground.

"So are we going hiking in the morning?" Riley asked.

"What do you mean by *morning*?" Garrett asked.

"And what do you mean by *hiking*?" Jenny added. "I came on this trip to relax, Riley."

"I'm in," Alex said. "What trail you want to try? West Canyon?"

"I was thinking of the incline trail, actually," Riley said amid a chorus of groans. "What? It's a good hike!"

And then, one by one, they all turned to watch a set of headlights coming. A small pickup truck rounded the corner. In another second a park ranger had climbed out.

"Evening," the man said.

"Everything okay?" Riley asked, standing. "We weren't making too much noise, were we?"

"No, nothing like that, kids. Is there an Alex Straker here?" the ranger asked.

Alex got to his feet, pulling Laura up with him. "I'm Alex," he croaked.

"Your mother called," the ranger said. "There's been an accident."

Chapter 17

Mark lay on the narrow, raised bed in the Royal Columbian Hospital, tubes and wires running from the various machines to his arms and chest. He was covered to his shoulders in a pale blue hospital blanket. A large white bandage covered one side of his head, the area around it shaved of hair.

On the chair beside the bed sat Mr. Straker, Mark's right hand clasped in both of his own, his eyes closed tightly. Although Alex couldn't hear the words his father murmured, he could see his lips moving.

As Alex stepped into the room, his father looked up, his face grey and terrified. "Alex, thank God you're here," he said.

"Where's Mom?" Alex asked. "She wasn't in the waiting room."

"No, she went to make a few more calls," Mr.

Straker said.

"What happened?"

"He and Scott were assaulted," Mr. Straker told him bluntly and Alex recoiled as though he'd just been hit himself. "Scott thought there were three of them but he isn't entirely sure."

"Is Scott in here, too?" Alex asked.

"No, he was checked over at Ridge Meadows Hospital and sent home with his mother." Mr. Straker wiped a hand across his mouth, a shadow passing across his features. "He only had a few scrapes and bruises. Mark sustained most of the injuries. Internal bleeding from blows to his stomach, a gash on his head ..." he stopped speaking and cleared his throat. "So he was brought here by ambulance."

Alex crossed the small stretch of linoleum and came to stand beside the bed. The hospital gown Mark wore had slipped. Alex leaned over and covered his brother's bare shoulder. Then he frowned, turning to his father.

"Where's Mark's cross?" he asked.

Mr. Straker looked at Mark's bare neck then back to Alex. "He didn't have it when they brought him into Ridge hospital. It must have fallen off."

"I'm sorry to disturb you," a nurse said softly from the doorway. "But they want to run a few tests. Would you mind going back to the waiting room for just a few minutes? We'll call as soon as we're done."

Mrs. Straker was sitting with Laura. She stood up as Alex and his dad entered the waiting room and hugged Alex, holding him so tightly he could barely breathe.

"Any change?" she asked, releasing him at last.

"No. He's still unconscious. They're just doing some more tests," Mr. Straker told her.

"They were minding their own business," Mrs. Straker said, fresh tears springing to her eyes. "Scott said they'd just stopped for coffee and were heading for the bus stop and these guys just appeared from nowhere! Who would do something like this? *Why* would someone do this?"

Kyle Jeffries, Alex thought. And suddenly he thought he might be sick. Muttering an apology he fled the waiting room, the heavy doors swinging behind him as he dashed to the water fountain. He leaned over the porcelain, wracked with dry heaves, hands braced above him on the brick wall.

Why hadn't he made sure Kyle knew Mark was his brother that night two weeks ago? Maybe if he had, Kyle wouldn't have dared try it again. What had stopped him? Had he really been more concerned with a teammate's opinion of him, a guy Alex didn't even *like*, than the safety of his own brother? A brother he *loved*.

This was Alex's fault. He could have stopped it. Should have stopped it. His brother was lying unconscious in the ICU because Alex had been too ashamed to stand up to a bully. He leaned his head against the wall, eyes burning.

"Alex?"

He cleared his throat, turning quickly. Scott stood in the hallway, staring at him with panic-stricken eyes.

"Oh my God, did something happen? Is Mark …" Fear filled Scott's voice.

"No, no, Mark's the same," Alex reassured him. "I just needed a drink."

Scott nodded, the panic fading from his eyes. Alex looked him over, taking in the sling cradling Scott's right arm, the scratches on his cheek, the bruise covering his left eye.

"Is he allowed to have visitors? Can I see him?" Scott's voice trembled as he spoke. "I need to see him."

"What happened, Scott?" Alex demanded. The public address system crackled and a doctor was paged. Two men, dressed in white coats, came out a door and walked past the boys, talking intently.

"You know what happened, Alex. I didn't see them coming until it was too late."

"It was the same guys, wasn't it?"

"Yeah, it was the same guys."

"I should have told Kyle Mark is my brother last time," Alex admitted. "I could have stopped it. But I didn't."

"No," Scott interrupted him, shaking his head vigorously. "No, it wasn't your fault, Alex. If anything it was my fault," he said, his face contorting in pain. "There was no one around," he whispered, "so I … I took Mark's hand. He didn't want to, kept shaking me off, but I insisted. I kept telling him we were alone and why couldn't we if we wanted to. And then they were there, calling us names and Mark was knocked to the ground. They kept kicking him!" Scott sank to the floor on his knees, sobs wracking him.

Alex knelt beside him on the dull linoleum floor. "You didn't do anything wrong," he said, patting Scott on the back awkwardly. "Listen. We're going to go to the cops," he went on, a plan forming as he spoke. "And we're going to tell them what happened and I'm going to tell them who it was. He's not going to get away with it."

Gradually Scott's tears slowed. He pulled away from Alex, wiping at his eyes. "Sorry, man, sorry," he muttered.

But Alex shook his head, his own throat rough with emotion. "Don't apologize." He helped Scott to his feet and they went back to the waiting room together.

Over the next hours they took turns going into the small cubicle with its pale walls and beeping machines to sit beside the unmoving patient. Through the rest of that long night and into the next morning they kept watch over Mark. The medical staff told them that they'd controlled the bleeding, that Mark was stable. Now they just had to wait for him to wake up.

***

Around mid-morning Laura took Mrs. Straker and Scott to the cafeteria to get something to eat. Alex had found a second chair and he and his father sat on either side of Mark, lost in their thoughts. Alex rested his head on the bed beside his brother's leg, eyes closed. He was so tired, beyond tired.

"Please, please, dear Lord," his father's voice whispered from across the bed. "Don't take my son. Don't take my beautiful boy. It doesn't matter that he's gay. Nothing else matters —"

Startled, Alex's head shot up. "You know?" he asked, interrupting the whispered words.

His father looked up at him, his face damp with tears. "Yes. I was suspicious before. But then, at Ridge hospital Scott let something slip and I knew for sure ..." He paused, let out a breath.

"And you don't care?"

"The only thing that matters is that my son is okay!" Mr. Straker cried, the pain in his voice filling the small, sterile room. He pulled a handkerchief from his pants' pocket and blew his nose, wiped his eyes. Then he got slowly to his feet.

"You stay with him," he ordered Alex and he slipped from the room.

Out in the corridor nurses walked softly, their voices hushed as they discussed patients. Visitors arrived for the elderly man in the room opposite Mark's and the curtains slid across the window. Mark's nurse, a man this morning, got up from his swivel chair and moved out of sight.

Left alone, Alex reached out and clasped Mark's hand as though they were about to arm wrestle. Mark had always fought so hard to beat his bigger brother, his face turning red with exertion, the muscles in his arms straining. And sometimes he had beat Alex, grinning like an idiot as he rubbed his shaking arm.

But this, this fight was too much for Mark to win on his own. He *had* to have help. "Lord," Alex began, not sure of the words he wanted, of the right words. "If you're there, if you're listening at all ..." Then suddenly the words did come, flowing from his heart. And he didn't care that he couldn't feel what he'd felt all his life. Mark believed, and he was doing this for Mark. And right now that was enough.

Epilogue

Alex hoisted himself up the ladder and swung under the low doorway of the tree house in one easy, fluid motion. He dropped down to the dusty floor then watched as Mark made his way cautiously up behind him. As he climbed, the hood of his sweater fell off his head, exposing the bristly black hairs just beginning to grow back. When his brother looked up, grinning, Alex saw the "J" shaped scar that ran, still red and raw-looking, across his forehead. It was the only visible scar his brother wore from his beating.

His brother's hand appeared at the top of the ladder and then his head and shoulders. Alex reached out and grabbed Mark's arm, tugging him gently through the narrow opening and into the tree house.

"Thanks, man," Mark said. He swung his legs over the open edge and sat, not speaking, while his breathing returned to normal.

"You ever clean this place?" he asked eventually, raising a dust-covered hand to Alex.

"Hard to find good help," Alex shot back. "You volunteering for the job?"

"You gonna install an elevator?"

Despite his brother's grin, Alex flinched at the subtle reference to Mark's injuries. Mark had opened his eyes later that second day, looking around at the faces of his mother and brother, confused by his surroundings, and their tear-streaked faces. And he'd been home from the hospital for a couple of weeks now. The doctors had said he could return to school when classes started next Tuesday, but all of them, Alex, their parents, even Scott, still hovered anxiously. He knew it drove his brother insane, but Alex, for one, couldn't help himself.

Alex leaned out the opening and grabbed a handful of leaves from an overhanging branch. Already the tips were touched with gold and crimson. Looking out across the back of their property he could see the flecks of brown and orange that polka-dotted the birch and maples. This summer had gone by as quickly as all the others, but unlike other years, Alex was not sorry to see it over.

Beside him Mark shifted his position and a quick flash of light caught Alex's attention. He turned and saw the silver chain hanging around his brother's neck.

"Hey, you got it back!" he said, indicating

the cross.

"Yeah. The police recovered it," Mark told him. He clasped the crucifix tightly in his hand and stared out over the trees.

"Dad told me they've charged Kyle and his gang with assault," Alex said.

Alex and Scott had gone together to the police station and had made their statements. It had been something concrete to do while Mark lay in a hospital bed. But Alex still carried the guilt of not having spoken up sooner.

"Yeah, we heard." Mark closed his eyes. "I wish they'd just let it go," he sighed.

"That's not going to happen, Mark," Alex said. "Whether it's labelled as a hate crime or not, it was a crime. He nearly killed you —"

"I know," Mark said, holding up his hand, stopping Alex's words. "I know."

Alex glanced down at the opening in the floor, at the ladder leading down to the ground, and then he turned back to Mark. "I haven't done a very good job of being your big brother this summer," he said slowly. "And I'm sorry."

"I know you are."

A thrush landed on a branch just outside of the tree house, its russet chest catching bits of light filtering through the leaves. It pecked at the bark, one glassy, black eye keeping watch on the brothers. Mark shifted and the thrush flew off.

"Laura told me you went to Mass with her while I was in the hospital," he said. He drew up his legs and leaned back against the wall, wrapping his arms around his knees.

Alex picked at a splinter of wood in the floor. "Yeah, a couple of times."

After that first time it hadn't been so hard, facing people. He was even able to shake hands with Paul Carruthers and not feel the urge to hit him. He couldn't control or change what other people did, and realizing that fact had actually been kind of a relief.

"And?" his brother pushed.

Alex shrugged. "Don't know. We'll see."

"It wasn't ever meant to be easy, Alex," Mark said.

"I know that."

"I think you want God to just present himself to you so you don't have to do any of the work," his brother said, watching Alex.

"You and Dad, with your perfect faith," Alex said.

Mark started laughing. "Perfect faith?" He grabbed the cross and pointed it at Alex. "You know why I lost this? I lost it because it wasn't around my neck. It was in my pocket and fell out when I got knocked to the ground." Alex frowned, confused.

"When I realized I was gay, like when I met Scott and knew for sure, I wanted to die. How could God have made me like that? It was easier to believe in no God at all than in one who would make me the way I am and then say I was a sinner."

"What changed for you?" Alex asked.

Mark looked up, brushed a hand across his eyes. "It was too overwhelming, the idea that we are alone in the universe."

Alex looked out across the yard where he and Mark had played as children: hide-and-seek among the trees and shrubs, pirates, flashlight tag. Those days seemed very far away now. Once, it had been as easy as believing what their parents told them: *Don't play with fire, you'll get burned. Just be yourself and people will like you. Have faith that God loves you.*

He glanced at Mark, sitting silently beside him. He'd rested his cheek on his arms and his eyes were closed. His brother looked so innocent and vulnerable, with his stubbly head and pale, exposed neck. But he wasn't an innocent little kid anymore; neither of them was, not anymore.

Now Alex knew that even if you *don't* play with fire you can get burned, that sometimes being yourself leaves you open to hatred, and that faith is a very fragile thing.

Next week he'd start his last year of high school. There were decisions to be made this year, choices to make. And yet, even with all the doubt and endless questions that seemed to go along with being at the edge of adulthood, there was something liberating in it all too.